DADDY'S CHRISTMAS ELF

ALI RYECART

To find out more about the author visit:
www.ryecart.com

Disclaimer

This book is a work of fiction. No part may be reproduced, by any means, by any electronic or mechanical means, including information storage and retrieval systems, without the written permission of the author, except for the use of brief quotations in a book review. Names and characters, businesses, organisations, products or services and places and events are either the product of the author's imagination or are used fictitiously. Any resemblance to actual persons, living or dead, is entirely coincidental.

All trademarks are the property of their respective owners.

© Ali Ryecart
2022

SYNOPSIS

**Take One Elf, Add an Older Man with Daddy Tendencies,
and Mix for the Perfect Christmas Romance**

Dressing up as a sexy little elf for a themed Christmas party isn't
Eli Turner's idea of a glittering career. It's the rowdiest event
Eli's worked this season and when a drunken proposition goes
too far, his refusal to play sets off a chain of events leaving him
high and dry with only the cheap elf suit on his back.

The Christmas party wealthy banker Grey Gillespie doesn't want
to be at is sliding out of control. When trouble erupts Grey
rushes to intervene, but not before the cute young guy dressed as
an elf flees and disappears into the freezing cold night.

The last thing Grey expects as he makes his way home is to
stumble across the little elf. Eli's dire predicament awakens
every one of Grey's deep-seated needs: to comfort, to protect, to
cherish and keep safe. Grey knows exactly what Eli yearns for
— his little elf just needs some gentle persuasion to understand
that everything he never knew he craved is everything Grey
desperately wants to give him.

*Daddy's Christmas Elf is a sweet with heat Daddy-lite
Christmas love story, oozing all the festive feels and fuzzies.
Hurt/comfort, forced proximity, age gap, and two men drawn
together to give the other exactly what he needs.*

DEDICATION &
ACKNOWLEDGEMENTS

Mark, thank you for your unstinting support and encouragement.

With thanks to Angela, Barbara, Sue, and Iola.

CHAPTER ONE

"That lot out there are a nightmare, but at least they're paying for their gropes." Santa pulled out a wad of notes from the front of his fur trimmed, red sequinned shorts; he counted it out and grinned. "But if it means I can get the nursery finished off and fully furnished by the time the baby comes in the New Year, they can squeeze as much as they like."

Eli's eyes opened wide. Was that a fifty pound note Santa stuffed back inside his shorts?

"At least you're getting something out of it, because all *I'm* getting is a sore arse. I've lost count of how many times it's been pinched. One guy even tried to put his hand down my legging but these things are so tight I'll have to be cut out of them at the end of the night." *Which can't come soon enough.*

Eli frowned down at himself, clad head to toe in green. Green leggings which left nothing to the imagination and were in danger of cutting off his blood supply, and a green fitted jacket which finished just above his crotch and made of horrible scratchy nylon which was making him itch. He got the costume, he understood it, he was after all one of Santa's Little Helpers, but the make-up? Wasn't that going too far?

Santa — Eli didn't know the guy's name — had told him to think of it as stage make-up. They were actors for the evening, and playing a part, he'd said as he applied eye shadow, eyeliner, and lipstick with what had looked to Eli like a practised hand. Eli's own attempts had been less sure. *Drunk drag queen isn't the look to go for*, one of the female Helpers had said with a laugh, as she wiped his face clean and re-applied his make-up. *Got to make the most of those eyes of yours.* She'd given him a smile and a wink as she shoved him in front of a mirror to take a look at himself.

The end result had been a surprise, and not an unpleasant one, but slap wasn't his thing. But he could hack it, like he could hack the ridiculous costume for a few hours, because the events company was paying good money for the Christmas season and the Santa's Little Helpers party, at a swanky West End hotel, was no exception. Eli needed every penny it paid. Loss of dignity, crushing embarrassment, and a sore arse was the price of a nice top-up to his savings account. He just wished somebody could get their hands down his front far enough to deposit a fifty pound note. Eli wrinkled his nose. Or maybe not.

"What are you doing here, wasting time? You should be out there working."

Eli and Santa both jumped and swung around as Sheena Jolly, the event planner, strode towards them.

"I'm not paying the two of you good money to stand

around gossiping. There are guests to serve. Who said you could take a break?"

"You did," Eli said, but the woman with the bad-tempered, scrunched-up face, and the long, swishy henna red hair wasn't haven't any of it.

"Desserts are about to be served, and we need everybody out there. Now." She glared at Eli, as though challenging him to argue.

Eli couldn't afford to argue. He nodded and straightened his hat, his very stupid hat with the bell dangling from its peak. The hat that was almost as stupid as his shoes with the long, curled up toes which also had a bell hanging from their ends. Tinkly little bells, like he was somebody's pet kitten. Thank god none of his friends could see him... But this gig, just like the others he'd worked, was all about the money. No, argument wasn't an option.

"Service!"

The event planner jerked her head towards the kitchen.

"Desserts are ready. Santa, you're now serving the top table. Elf, you know your tables. Get to it. Gillespie Associates is a new and highly valued client, so everything needs to be as smooth as silk. No cock ups." With a swish of her swishy hair, Sheena turned on her heel and clattered away.

"Service! Get an elfin' move on!"

"Let's get on with it. I can't afford to piss her off," Santa muttered under his breath as they made their way to the kitchen to collect the desserts.

Eli's stomach rumbled. He hadn't eaten since breakfast, before it had even got light, and it was now almost 8.30pm. He'd hoped to be able to snag something to eat from the kitchen but he, like everybody else, had been flat out since arriving at the hotel that morning to help set up the themed party.

Eli huffed as he picked up the tray laden with four large plates, each holding a selection of Christmas treats artfully arranged in the centre. Mini Christmas pudding, mince pie, and stollen, all of them sweet and warm and accompanied by a large jug of brandy-laced cream. His stomach rumbled again and his mouth watered. Sure, he'd be able to eat at the end of the evening, but midnight, when the corporate Christmas party was due to finish, might as well have been weeks away.

Santa pushed through the door into the function room, and Eli followed.

The noise, which for a few blessed minutes had been muted, hit him full in the face. He was sure it'd got noisier and even more raucous. The party guests, a firm of City investment bankers, were the rowdiest he'd worked over the Christmas season. Everybody he'd come into contact with that night had been tanked up on the free-flowing booze, which had not only loosened inhibitions but had ripped them off and chucked them away. Eli had held his tongue, his smile fixed on his face. He'd been leered at, touched up and propositioned by both men and women. He wouldn't have minded so much if it had all been accompanied by bank notes stuffed down his front... Or he'd have minded less. Maybe.

Just think about the money. Remember why you're doing this. The words he said to himself before every gig. All he needed to do was Keep Calm and Carry On — just like it said on his morning coffee mug.

Eli sucked in a deep breath and widened his smile, hoping it didn't look too much like a grimace.

"Desserts, ladies and gentlemen." *Just keep smiling.*

This was the worst of the tables assigned to him. Louder, rowdier, and way ruder than the others put together, with the loudest, rowdiest, rudest guy of the lot smirking as he looked Eli up and down. Again.

"Well, it's our very own sexy little elf. Love the lip gloss, by the way." The guy's smirk grew wider. "You look like you're an extra in an adults-only seasonal special."

The guy's comment drew drunken laughter from the others around the table.

"Your dessert, madam." Eli put a plate in front of a glassy-eyed woman, ignoring the remark. "Cream?"

She shook her head and instead refilled her wine glass, sloshing it over the side.

Eli made his way around the table, serving the women first. The smirking guy said nothing more as the conversation resumed. Eli gave a silent sigh of relief. The guy had been goading him all evening, but now he seemed to have forgotten about him. One more tray of desserts to bring out and then he could move on to serving his other tables. Eli poured cream for the last of the women he'd served and was about to put the jug on the table when a hand tightened around his arm. Eli yelped as he was tugged down into the smirking guy's lap.

"What do you think you're doing? You can't do this. Let me go."

"Stop being a twat and leave the kid alone," one of men muttered. His attention flickered from his dessert to Eli and back again, where it settled, Eli all but forgotten.

"It's just a bit of fun. It's Christmas, and isn't Christmas all about having fun? What do you think, elf?"

The guy's grin turned to a leer.

Feral.

Eli's heart beat faster. If this had been a dark street, he'd have run as far and fast as he could, but the guy, thin and wiry but strong, held him fast.

"You're Santa's Little Helper, aren't you? How about helping me with this."

"Ehhg! Fuck off, you slimy creep," Eli burst out when the guy ground his erection against his arse.

Eli tried to push himself away, but the guy had him pinned down. Somebody — another elf, Santa, the event planner, anybody — had to come and help, but amidst the noise and drunken laughter, everybody was oblivious to what was happening.

"For god's sake, Murray, that's enough," the glassy-eyed woman slurred.

"We're only having a laugh, aren't we?" The guy called Murray grinned wider.

Eli lurched backwards as he tried to get away, jarring his back against the edge of the table. Pain burned through him, along with anger.

"Pass the jug, I want cream," the drunk woman muttered.

"We all want cream, don't we?" Murray sniggered as he ran his hand up Eli's thigh, towards where Eli's jacket stopped just short of his crotch.

Eli shoved Murray's hand away, his anger turning to white hot rage. No way was he taking this crap.

"You want cream? You can fucking have it."

Eli didn't have time to wince with pain as he twisted

and grabbed the jug just before the woman pulled it towards her. With one hand, Eli swung the heavy jug in an arc — and emptied it over Murray's head.

Eli was almost catapulted from Murray's lap as thick cream dripped from Murray's soaked head all over his shoulders and down the front of his suit.

The drunken laughter and chatter around the table fell silent.

"You little bastard. Can't you take a joke? What the fuck do you think you're playing at?" Murray was panting hard, his sharp teeth bared in a snarl. Eli swallowed. The guy looked like a rabid dog, ready to attack.

Those at the tables nearest to them began to turn and stare, the start of a tidal wave of attention Eli wanted to run away from. He was shaking. From his turned up at the toes ridiculous shoes with the bells hanging from the ends, to the bell topped tip of his equally stupid felt hat, every part of Eli was shaking as fury and humiliation consumed him.

"What was *I* playing at? Stopping you from rubbing your nasty little dick all over my bum, for a start. That's assault, and I'm going to report you to the police."

Even as Eli's threat fell from his lips, he knew it was pointless. Who around the table would back his word against their slimeball colleague's?

Murray's answering sneer sent a fresh wave of anger through Eli. He pulled his shoulders back, tilted his chin up, gathering together as much dignity as a man dressed as an elf could, as he let his words ring out.

"If you're so desperate to get your rocks off, there are plenty of dark back streets around here where you can do it for a price."

The collective gasp was louder than any of the raucous laughter Eli had been hearing all night.

Murray's face, through the curtain of cream, turned blood red. He lunged forward as Eli staggered back, and everything exploded into fast forward.

Sheena, the sour faced events planner, hurtled forward like a bullet, a couple of minions on her heels, as she darted between Eli and Murray.

"I'm so sorry for this unacceptable and outrageous behaviour. I can't apologise enough for what's happened. Let me—" Sheena began to dab at Murray's ruined suit.

"What?" Eli's head snapped from Murray to Sheena. "He was touching me up — he had no right. What was I supposed—?"

"Please leave the function room, Elias." Two small, angry eyes bored into him. "Now."

"But he was—"

"What's going on here?" The voice cut across Eli, from behind him, clipped but calm and full of authority.

"He tried—"

"Elias! Wait for me in the staff area. Now."

Eli didn't need to be told twice. Spinning around and almost falling over his stupid shoes, he dipped his head and did everything he could to stop himself from running.

CHAPTER TWO

"...but he was rubbing himself off on me, for god's sake. That's assault. I could go to the police. I could sue him." Could he? Eli had no idea about the suing, but he was on a roll. And furious, so bloody furious at the injustice of it all.

"I don't see a long line of witnesses queuing up to back your version of events." Sheena raised an over-plucked brow at the same time she swished her hair. "You caused a scene, in front of a very prestigious and valued client. It is not," she said, stabbing at each word, "the sort of behaviour Jolly Eventful expects from those who work for the company. Even casual staff." She said the words with sniff.

She's washing her hands of this, she's not going to do anything...

"What about your duty of care? To your employees?"

"But you're not an employee, are you? You're a casual seasonal worker with no rights beyond your agreed hourly rate."

"What he did, it was assault!" Eli hated the wobble in

his voice and the shake, now the adrenaline that had flooded his system was receding, which travelled from the top of his head to the tip of his toes.

Sheena flapped her hand, as though Eli were no more than an irksome fly. "It's best you leave, because I have quite enough to deal with without you causing extra work. I'm willing to pay you for the remainder of the evening, as a gesture of goodwill. You'll receive an additional three hours' pay, for which you'll not have worked." Her face screwed up as though she were in physical pain.

Eli blinked. And blinked again.

"Leave? You're sacking me? But I was being—"

"*I* am being very lenient. *You* assaulted a client. God alone knows what the dry cleaning bill will be. Elias, please go and get changed, and collect your things. If you haven't left within—" she looked at her watch, "fifteen minutes, I will have no option but to ask security to escort you from the premises."

"*What?*" But it was too late, as Sheena, kitten heels tapping out a bad-tempered tattoo, flicked and swished her hair as she walked away.

Eli stared after her. He could... He could what? There was nothing he could do, and he knew it as much as Sheena did. He was hourly paid casual staff to be hired and fired at will, whatever the circumstances, just as Sheena effin' Jolly had made very clear. What was left of his anger and indignation flooded out of him. He was tired and fed up, his only option to pack up and go, and wave goodbye to any more work from Jolly Eventful.

At least I won't have to dress up like a slutty elf again.... Or a banana, which he'd been at the Festival of Fruit in the summer.

The changing room was empty and silent, and Eli made his way over to the battered locker in the corner.

Oh no. No, no, no…

Could his evening get any worse?

The door to the locker was ajar and Eli pulled it fully open. His heart fell. His jeans, jumper, jacket, boots — all of them gone. The jacket that had his wallet in, his phone, his keys, his travel card…

The padlock lay on the floor, partially hidden by the bench, as though it'd been hurriedly kicked away, and he swooped to pick it up.

Eli had worked enough functions and events to always check he securely locked his stuff away as thefts from hotel staff changing rooms were common. But this time he'd been running late, getting to the hotel with only seconds to spare, Sheena berating him and threatening to dock his pay. He'd been flustered as Miss Swishy Hair had been on and on at him, her braying bad-tempered words battling the awkward, cringing conversation he'd had with his flat mate Benny that morning, a conversation that had been going around in his head on a continuous loop, a conversation he'd been half expecting and wholly dreading.

Had he snapped the padlock closed properly? He had his answer as he stared at the bronze coloured lock. There were no signs of damage; it hadn't been forced, just like the hasp on the locker door hadn't.

Eli sank down onto the bench and let his head fall into his hands.

How the hell was he going to get home? Covent Garden to Stockwell. It wasn't *that* far, only around three miles, but anywhere was too far when dressed as an elf…

Eli shuddered. Maybe Sheena would give him an advance so he could get a cab? *Yeah, some hope.*

The changing room door flew open. A heavily built security guard, his ill-fitting uniform barely containing his bulk, glared at Eli.

"You go now," the guard said, in heavily accented English. "I take you off hotel."

"My stuff's been stolen. I've got to report it to the manager."

"Who care? Hotel full. Manager too busy. And he do fuck all," the guard said, adding a derisive snort.

Eli's spirits dropped even further, because the burly guard was right. The hotel was heaving, because the Jolly Eventful party wasn't the only one taking place that night, and the misfortunes of a fired elf weren't going to be top of the hotel manager's list. Eli blinked away the sudden sting of tears, as every star in the universe aligned against him.

"I'm going to have to borrow some chef's whites, or some other uniform, because I can't leave looking like this." Eli stood up and waved an arm over himself, but the security guard just shrugged.

"The woman, with face like old prune, she tell me to take you off hotel." The guard rolled his shoulders and cracked his knuckles before taking a step forward.

"Okay, okay. I'm going." Eli stumbled back. He didn't fancy being assaulted for a second time in one night.

"We go through car park. Is quickest. My break start in one minute." The guard scowled as he beckoned Eli forward.

Eli groaned. What choice did he have? At least people

12

would probably think he was on his way to a Christmas fancy dress party. Eli followed the chunky guard through a maze of narrow corridors, to a door which the guard unlocked. It opened onto the underground car park. It was small, with maybe no more than a dozen cars. A keen wind whistled through and Eli shivered after the warmth of the hotel.

"I put you on street, out of hotel," the guard growled.

"Thought your break was starting."

The guard stopped and looked at Eli from over one beefy shoulder, his face scrunched up in thought.

"They don't pay me for break." He jerked his head towards an upwards slope and an EXIT sign at the far end of the car park. "You go."

A moment later the door slammed closed and the lock turned.

"Fuck. Fuck, fuck, fuck."

Eli wrapped his arms around himself as a fresh gust of wind blew through the car park. He was already starting to shiver. His feet, protected from the rough concrete flooring by nothing more than the thin fabric of the ridiculous shoes, were already hurting as sharp pieces of grit dug into the soles of his feet.

Tears of frustration, impotent anger, and out and out hopelessness finally overflowed and Eli dragged the back of a hand across his eyes. The day had started badly and had gone downhill fast. And in the New Year, he was going to have to look for somewhere new to live. He drew in a shuddering breath. Get moving, get home — for as long as it was home. It'd take ages as he had no option but to walk, but he'd be rewarded with something to eat and a hot bath before he raided Benny's not so secret stash of top-end vodka. Eli's lips lifted in a tiny smile, the only good thought to come out of today.

Happy Christmas, Benny. Happy fucking Christmas.

The thought was a faint ember of warmth in Eli's chest as he threaded through the cars towards the exit.

One car stood out amongst the rest. Larger, sleeker, shinier and polished to within an inch of its life. Eli didn't know much about cars, but this one screamed classic — otherwise known as old. He also knew the emblem rearing up on the front, a tiger, or maybe a puma, meant it was a very expensive one. Or maybe it was a… *Of course, it's a Jag.*

He glanced through the window as he passed, nothing more than quick and cursory. And stopped.

The car was unlocked, the little buttons standing proud.

On the back seat was a coat. A thick winter coat. And a scarf.

A fresh blast of wind blew through the car park, freezing Eli down to his bones.

A coat, and a scarf… Eli licked his lips. His eyes darted around the deserted car park. No sign of anybody or anything. Except a coat and a scarf, and he needed both.

No.

Eli shook his head and took a step forward, towards the slope and the EXIT sign. He wasn't a thief and he wasn't going to become one.

Another gust of wind, cold enough to freeze the blood in his veins.

Eli's hand was on the rear door handle before he could stop himself. He could leave a note, telling whoever the coat and scarf belonged to that they'd be returned to the hotel. He was only borrowing, not stealing, that was all. He was only doing it because he was desperate.

Eli lunged at the coat, and dragged it towards him. It was heavy, the wool silky soft, everything about it was expensive. A bubble of doubt burst in his stomach. What the hell was he doing? No way could he do this. He let the coat drop from his hand, but a sudden loud scraping noise, and voices, burst from the opening door, the one the security guard had slammed shut on him.

Panic seized Eli and he froze. The Jag's back door was wide open, he was more inside it than not, his arse sticking high in the air. And he was in full view of the tall, thin man standing in the doorway, and dressed in a chauffeur's uniform. The guy was side on to him, and all it would take would be a slight turn of the head and a few strides and Eli would be caught red handed.

"Thanks, Sergei. Have a happy Christmas." The chauffeur waved goodbye, and began to turn.

It was too late to scramble out and run. Eli did the only thing he could. Throwing himself head first onto the back seat, he pulled the door to a close a split second before the chauffeur made his way across, as Eli slipped into the footwell and rolled himself into a ball.

CHAPTER THREE

Grey set his face in neutral and stared. He didn't have to say a word, or move a muscle. All he needed to do was stare. The trick had been perfected years before and most times Grey was barely aware he was using it. But he was aware now, as Murray squirmed, as he protested he was the innocent party, as he stumbled out his pathetic excuses for being a drunk, lecherous bully before falling into a cowed silence.

Just a couple of months before, Murray had been a less than stellar appointment to Gillespie Associates and he was hanging on by a thread. Or he had been until this evening. Now the thread had been cut and the only reason he would return in the New Year would be to remove his personal belongings in a small cardboard box.

"I suggest, Murray, that you get yourself cleaned up and leave."

Grey had no need to raise his voice to make his point, the icy hard edge beneath the calm, level words did more than a good enough job. He smiled, and Murray's face blanched, making him as pale as the cream that continued to drip down from his head. The little elf, who'd since fled, had made sure he'd tipped every drop out.

Murray nodded, and all but ran from the function room. If one good thing had come out of tonight's events, it was that he didn't have to see Murray ever again; a brief email to his Director of HR would see to that.

With Murray's departure, the chatter and the chink of glasses resumed, as though it were a collective exhale of breath. The piped music, which had been playing in the background during dinner, was turned up as though to plaster over the crack in the evening.

"I must apologise, Mr. Gillespie."

Grey had forgotten about the event planner, who hovered at his elbow.

"What for?" His words were blunt, and she jerked back.

"The… the seasonal member of staff. He's a casual—"

"I fail to see what his employment status has to do with what happened."

The woman — Grey couldn't recall her name, if he'd known it in the first place as the party had been delegated to his PA to organise — inclined her head a fraction and clasped her hands together.

"I wish to assure you that Jolly Eventful would never, ever, have somebody who was so volatile on the permanent staff. At Jolly Eventful, we expect our employees to handle all and any situation with calm professionalism. The person who was the cause of this unfortunate incident is no longer working for us, in any capacity."

Grey was about to return to the table where his senior team sat, but her words stopped him. She was smiling up at him, if her scrunched expression could be called that.

"I beg your pardon?"

"The casual employee," she said, emphasising the words, as though distancing herself and her party planning company from the whole affair, "will not, I can assure you, be undertaking any further work with us."

She was still scrunching her face up at Grey.

"You mean you've dismissed him? When he was clearly the injured party? From what I saw, he was sorely provoked into taking action. A casual, seasonal worker or not, don't you think Jolly Eventful had a duty of care towards him?"

"I—yes, but—"

The woman squirmed, as Grey knew she would.

"I… Of course. Jolly Eventful takes very seriously—"

Grey turned away, uninterested in anything else the woman had to say, leaving her to bluster and stumble out her excuses into thin air.

Grey had seen, too late, what had been going on, pushing to his feet just as the elf had grabbed hold of the jug of cream and up-ended it over Murray. He'd been ordered away and was no doubt long gone, the ridiculous costume left behind as he'd got changed and fled. The awful Ms. Jolly may have been the one to do the firing but it had been Grey's now former employee who'd been the cause of him losing his job. Grey let out a long, deep sigh. The little elf who'd all but run for his life was owed compensation, if not by Jolly Eventful then by Gillespie Associates, and he made a mental note to instruct his PA to make it happen.

A band was setting up on the small stage, marking the next stage of the evening. He'd only intended to stay for the dinner, not that he'd wanted to attend even that, but as the CEO of Gillespie Associates, one of London's most up and coming private banking firms, it had been expected; the band's appearance, however, was his cue to escape. Making his goodbyes, and wishing his senior team with whom he'd shared a table a Merry Christmas, Grey slipped out of the function room, closing the door behind him just as the MC for the evening began to introduce the band.

Grey puffed out a long breath, and leaned against the door. His dark blond hair, which now, he'd noticed in the mirror recently, was increasingly threaded with silver, flopped over his brow. Grey pushed it away and rubbed his forehead in an attempt to massage away the faint beginnings of a headache. Tonight had been a strain, even without Murray's drunken exploits. Grey was out of practise when it came to socialising, not that he'd been much of one for parties and other large social gatherings to begin with.

And hadn't that been a handy stick to beat me with…

He shoved himself away from the door, and rolled his shoulders before he pulled them back. *That* part of his life was over with, and he refused to prod and pick at the wound which had barely had time to scab over. Or he refused to pick at it most of the time. He shook his head, short and hard. No point in looking back when he needed to look forward. The only problem was, forward seemed to point to nothing other than a featureless infinity.

Maybe he should have his driver drop him off at a bar on the way home. He knew a couple of places which were smart and low key, where the propositions were discreet and the cost of an evening's companionship, or even just a few minutes, was obliquely agreed to over expensive cocktails, nobody brazen enough to say what the other was.

The thought left him as cold as a blast of Arctic wind. No, he'd go home, open up the fine brandy he'd saved for Christmas even if Christmas was technically still a few days away, and instead give himself up to the winsome, four legged charms of Trevor.

Grey pulled his phone from the inside pocket of his suit jacket; the call was picked up before the second ring.

"I'm ready to be taken home now, Colin... Yes, I'll see you outside the front of the hotel." Grey cut the call. If Colin was surprised by the early hour, it didn't show in his voice.

Grey stepped out of the hotel, just as Colin was gliding towards him in the vintage sleek, black Jag. Grey shivered as a hard wind blew. When had it got this cold? The temperature had dropped by several degrees in just a couple or so hours, he was sure of it. He hadn't bothered taking his coat into the hotel, leaving it on the back seat rather than checking it in.

"Mr. Gillespie." Colin tapped the peak of his chauffeur's cap as he jumped out from the driver's seat and opened the door for Grey to climb into the back. Grey smiled his thanks. He could just as well have opened the door himself, but Colin was old school, and would have seen it as a slight on his professionalism.

Settling himself into the soft leather seat as the Jag eased its way into the Friday night traffic, all Grey wanted to do was get home and shut the door on the evening. Shifting a leg, he knocked against something solid. He looked down — and met a pair of wide, terrified eyes staring up at him.

"Colin?"

"Yes, Mr. Gillespie?"

"We seem to have acquired an elf."

CHAPTER FOUR

"I'm so sorry, Mr. Gillespie, I don't understand—"

"No, Colin, it's quite all right." Grey raised his hand, and the chauffeur stepped back from the open door. They'd pulled up on the side of the road. Colin was flustered, embarrassed at the appalling slip in professionalism which had allowed an elf to curl up in the footwell.

Grey extended his hand. "Let me help you up."

"S'okay." The elf uncurled himself, hauled himself upright, and fell sideways onto the back seat.

"I'll call the police, Mr. Gillespie. This person must have been planning to steal—"

"I'm not a thief! And I wouldn't be in here if you'd have done your job properly and locked the car when you went for a wee."

The elf glared at Colin, who went quiet, and Grey dipped his head to hide the grin that twitched at his lips. But it fell away almost immediately.

Grey had recognised the elf immediately. The boy — he'd looked no more than about eighteen or nineteen when

Grey had seen him in the function room — was clearly a little older than he'd first appeared but not by much. It was probably why he'd got the job as a Christmas elf, a Christmas elf who was now an unemployed elf, as a result of Murray's unacceptable, crass, drunken behaviour.

"Why were you crouching in the back of the car?"

"I, erm…" The elf slumped and his shoulders drooped. Chewing on his lower lip, he peered up at Grey, desolation filling his eyes, lovely big eyes that were—

"It's called heterochromia," the elf mumbled.

"I know what it's called." Eyes of different colours, in this case one grey, the other green. Rare, and in the elf's case, utterly captivating.

"Mr. Gillespie?"

Grey dragged his gaze from the elf to the chauffeur, who raised his brows in question. Grey cleared his throat, as he looked back at the elf.

"You haven't answered my question."

"I—I saw your coat on the back seat." The elf looked down at the coat, which lay between them. "I also saw the door was unlocked — when it shouldn't have been." The elf glared at Colin, before he slid his gaze back to Grey. "I was sacked, because I wouldn't put up with your employee having his hands all over me." The elf tilted his chin up and locked his gaze to Grey's, pride and self respect in the gesture. "But when I went to get changed, my locker had been ransacked and all my stuff was gone. I was going to borrow the coat, that's all, and bring it back to the hotel. I mean, look at me. Do you really think I can make my way home dressed like this?"

The elf opened his arms wide, and Grey had to concede the point.

A lurid green suit, so tight it could have been spray painted on, clung to every lean muscle. And as for the make up… Dark eyeliner smudged the skin beneath his captivating, mesmerising eyes, eyes that needed no cosmetics to make them stand out. Deep red lipstick painted a pair of generous, pouty lips, but it was smeared across the elf's mouth, as though somebody had taken possession of those lips and kissed him long and hard. The boy, with his large, clear eyes and red-smeared mouth, looked at the same time both innocent and debauched.

Heat prickled over Grey's skin as a tingle raced the length of his spine. He cleared his throat and sat up straighter.

"I can only apologise for what happened," Grey said, his voice too loud and formal. "Had I realised what was happening I'd have intervened sooner. If it's any kind of consolation, he won't be returning to his job in the New Year. I know the event planner dismissed you, and although I can't force her to re-instate you, I can however arrange some measure of financial compensation for what happened."

The elf jolted back, his eyes widening.

"Why would you do that? It wasn't your fault—"

"My employee — or former employee — caused you to be fired so it was to some degree my fault, even if only vicariously. But, for now, you need to get home, so let my driver take you."

"Wow. Thank you, but you've no need—"

"There's every need."

A flush flooded the elf's face. He looked up at Grey through beautiful, captivating eyes. With his dark hair peeking out from under the felt hat, *elfin* was the perfect description.

"I don't know what to say… But a lift would be good. It's bloody freezing."

"Colin." Grey looked at the chauffeur, whose professionalism slipped as he stared at Grey as though he'd lost his mind. "We're taking a detour to…?" Grey turned to the elf.

"Stockwell."

Across the Thames and the polar opposite direction to where Grey lived, in Hampstead. He could give him some money for a cab and even the loan of his coat, yet turfing the elf out of the car, after the disastrous night he'd had, to make his own way home didn't sit easy with Grey.

"That's not a problem. Colin, if you wouldn't mind?"

"Mr. Gillespie," the chauffeur said, his professional demeanour back in place, as he gave a brisk nod and climbed back into the driver's seat.

"Thank you," the elf said as he buckled up. "The last Friday night before Christmas isn't the best time to be out on the street, dressed like something from an extra in an adults-only seasonal special, as your employee put it."

"Ex-employee." Grey said it automatically, his brain suddenly preoccupied with thoughts of what that seasonal special might entail. *What the—?* Maybe he should get Colin to drop him off at the bar, after all. "What's your name?" Hadn't the prune-faced event planner said? He couldn't call the guy Elf, even if the name did suit him.

"Elias Turner. Eli for short, and it's what everybody calls me. I think my parents were having a particularly sick joke when they landed me with that name. My middle one's even worse. Kestrel."

"Elias, or Eli's, fine. But — excuse me?"

Eli couldn't have said what Grey thought he had. Could he?

"Kestrel."

Yes, Grey had heard right.

Eli was scrutinising him as though he expected him to laugh. Grey met Eli's gaze and didn't flinch. "It is, let's say, a somewhat unusual name."

Eli shook his head and laughed softly. In the dim light in the back of the car, it sent a shiver through every one of Grey's nerve endings.

"That's one way of putting it. The other is that my parents, grungy old hippies the pair of them, had smoked too much weed on the day they had to register my birth. Reckon I'd change it by deed poll if I could ever be bothered to get around to it."

Eli rested his head against the window and stared out at the crowded streets, but his eyelids soon fluttered to a close.

Grey cast regular glances Eli's way, careful for his gaze not to linger too long. He'd asked for Eli's name, but disappointment scratched at him that Eli hadn't asked in return.

As the car pushed its way through the traffic, Grey thought about the pile of work he could get through over the next few days when the firm was closed for the Christmas and New Year break. He'd be spending the Season of Goodwill alone, so what difference did it make if he chose to work when everybody else was celebrating with their families and loved ones? A spasm of regret and sadness shuddered through him.

How could his life have changed so radically and irretrievably in just over a year? Grey squirmed, crossing and uncrossing his long legs. He'd marked, only a month ago, the anniversary of the start of the decline by drinking far too much and failing miserably with the escort he'd hired for the night. It was supposed to have been a stark message to himself, if nobody else, that he had moved on. Instead it had been demeaning and embarrassing, the loss of control so alien to his nature, that he'd thrust a huge tip at the guy, doubling his rate for the night, before all but shoving him out the door.

"Mr. Gillespie?"

Grey started. They were already crossing the Thames at Vauxhall bridge, and they'd be in Stockwell within minutes. He'd been so caught up in memories, he'd not noticed the journey. Of course, Colin would need Eli's address. Grey shook Eli's arm to wake him. Eli looked around him, blinking as wakefulness came back to him.

"Oh. Right. We're nearly there." He leaned forward and gave Colin the address. A right turn, a left and a left again, and the car came to a stop in a small street lined with terraced houses. "Thanks, I appreciate the lift."

Eli unbuckled his seatbelt, hesitating before he opened the car door.

"I was only going to borrow your coat because I was desperate, and I would've returned it, I swear. But I wouldn't have taken it back to the hotel because I doubt you'd have seen it again. Hotels are terrible places for theft. I'd have found your work address and taken it there."

Eli's two-coloured eyes rested on Grey's, the same proud tilt to his chin as earlier.

"I believe you."

Eli smiled, and there was something bashful about it,

and suddenly it was as though he was the teenager Grey had first mistaken him for.

"I never asked your name, did I?"

No. "Grey. Grey Gillespie."

Eli's brows lifted. "Grey? Were your parents stoned old hippies, too?"

Grey laughed, throwing his head back. Eli couldn't have been more wrong.

"Anything but. One an accountant, the other a maths teacher." Good people both, yet they could have done with more than a little hippy to warm their chilly blood.

Eli's smile turned into a grin. "Goodnight, Grey. And thanks again. Happy Christmas."

A second later, Eli was gone, and bounding towards a short set of steps leading to a front door.

"Home, Mr. Gillespie?"

"Yes, thank you Colin."

The car glided away from the kerb, and Grey resisted the temptation to twist around and look out of the back window before the car turned a corner and they made for the main road and all points north of the river.

CHAPTER FIVE

"You have got to be joking. I don't believe it, I don't fucking believe it."

Eli looked under the mat. He looked under the plant pots that framed the steps leading up to the front door. He looked under the gnome. Again. And then he did it *again.*

The key. Where was the frigging key? But Eli knew, he just knew.

Lenny. It had to be. Benny wouldn't have deliberately removed it. Or at least Eli didn't think he would…

Ever since moving in, Lenny — Benny's boyfriend — had been bitching about Eli and Benny's habit of hiding a door key outside. Maybe keeping it under a bloody gnome wasn't exactly smart thinking, but they'd never had any trouble during the two years Eli had been Benny's lodger.

He wasn't to know I'd get my stuff nicked… But what Lenny did know was that Eli had a habit of letting the front door slam shut, only then to remember he'd left his keys in his room. Or in the kitchen. Or the bathroom. It was why he and Benny had put a spare under the gnome in the first place, the gnome whose cheeky smile now looked like a smug leer. *I might only be a cheap plaster gnome, but you're a sad loser.*

And that was exactly what he'd been today, a day when nothing had gone right. Well, one thing had, or kind of.

The lift home in the warm and comfy Jag, with the hot as fuck Grey Gillespie. Hot as fuck, in his dark suit that must have been made for him, as it showed off his broad shoulders and long, slim legs. But his luck had once again run its pathetic, short course as the car had slipped away and turned the corner, taking it and the very tasty Grey out of sight and out of his life.

Eli hammered at the door again, but it was pointless. Benny and Lenny, who were starting to sound less and less like a comedy duo, would be in Austria by now, getting pissed on glühwein and stuffing their faces with whatever you stuffed your face with in Austria. They were away for the whole festive season and when they got back, Benny would be expecting Eli to pack his bag, turning the little terraced house into a love nest for two instead of a gooseberry patch for three.

"Shit."

Eli dropped to the step and let his head hang, wracking his brain for what to do next. He had nowhere to go. Family and friends, they weren't anywhere nearby, and with no phone he couldn't contact them in any case. He looked at the houses either side of the terrace. Like Benny's place, they were in darkness, the owners finding someplace better than the small, tucked away South London street in which to spend the festive season.

There was only one thing he could do, and the second time he'd considered breaking the law within the last couple of hours. He'd have to smash a window and break in. Was it technically breaking in, if he lived in the house? Even if he wasn't the owner? He didn't know but what choice did he have?

It all went around and around in Eli's head as he hunched on the step. Whatever he did, he had to make up his mind soon because it was getting colder by the second and his teeth were beginning to chatter. As if on cue, the first snow flakes began to fall, the prelude for the heavy overnight downfall the weather forecaster on the telly had promised.

Eli had no choice, because tonight had been all about no choice after no choice. He pushed himself up, ready to make his way to the rickety fence further along the street. He'd climb over it and hope he didn't fall and break his neck as he dropped into the narrow private alleyway that ran behind the short row of terraces, clogged up with the householders' refuse bins. He'd use those to get himself over Benny's back garden fence, smash a window and get in the house — and pay a fortune for a glazier to come out to fix it before Benny got home.

The snow began to fall in earnest, urging him on. If his luck carried on the way it'd been going today, somebody would see him and call the police.

Officer, there's an elf breaking in to one of the houses...

Eli laughed, but it was edged with hysteria, as he made his way down the steps, made slippery by the falling snow.

A car, the only thing moving on the street, pulled to a stop in front of the house. A sleek, black, classic car with the pouncing jaguar on the bonnet. The window glided down.

"Eli?"

Eli blinked, as much out of surprise as the snow blowing into his eyes. What was Grey doing back here? Eli picked his way over, wincing as freezing cold, wet snow soaked through his felt shoes. He leaned down to look at Grey.

"Are you lost? Is the sat nav not working?" The warmth that leached from the open window over his cold skin made him want to climb back in the car, rather than over the old wooden fence, and curl up, preferably against Grey, but he'd take the footwell.

"No. I wanted to check that you got in without any trouble. I should have waited."

"Why? Were you hoping to come in for coffee? Only joking." But if Grey had suggested it, Eli didn't think he'd have said no. Although, the way things were going, he wasn't going to be inviting anybody in for anything.

"Why are you still out here?"

"The spare key we always kept hidden, it's been removed." *Thank you, Lenny, thank you very much.*

"You're locked out? Is there anybody who can put you up for the night I can take you to?"

Eli shook his head, dislodging flakes of snow that had settled on him and setting the bell on this cap jingling. "My parents live on a remote Scottish island with a herd of smelly goats, and any friends I could ask are away. Thanks for coming back, I appreciate it, but I've got to find a way in before I freeze to death."

"Break in, you mean?"

"I prefer to think of it as an alternative means of entry." Eli glanced away, as embarrassment swept over him. He'd been the victim tonight, but it was the second time he'd been caught by Grey straddling the line between right and wrong. "I've got no choice." Eli turned back to Grey. "The alternative is to find a sheltered doorway to sleep in, but I'll wake up with the same situation on my hands." If he did wake up. The temperature had plummeted further and the snow was coming down heavier than ever. "Sorry, but I've got to go."

"Get in the car."

Eli stopped in mid-turn. He'd already told Grey there was nobody he could call upon, and a flare of irritation burst inside him.

"I've already said—"

"I heard what you said, and I'm saying get in the car. You've nowhere else to go, and you're contemplating breaking in. And you're soaked. You can stay with me tonight. I've got plenty of spare room."

Eli cocked his head to the side. "Why? You don't know me. Aren't you afraid I might eat every mince pie you have in the house before nicking the family silver and making off into the night?" Oh, it was tempting to say yes to Grey, so, so tempting. And he did kind of know Grey, didn't he? Or sort of.

Grey's lips twisted in a gloomy smile as he shrugged one shoulder. "In that costume? I don't think you'd get very far. I feel a sense of responsibility for what's happened to you. The very least I can do is put you up tonight, and help you on your way tomorrow. But it's your choice."

Eli bit down on his lip. His predicament wasn't Grey's fault at all, but as an icy gust of wind cut through him, he knew there was only one choice to be made. Dashing around to the other passenger door, Eli wrenched it open and jumped inside.

CHAPTER SIX

Closing the front door on the winter weather, Grey looked down at Eli.

"You need a change of clothes."

Although Eli had dried off a little in the journey across London, he was still soaked and the elf costume, already tight on Eli, clung to him even more. What had Eli said Murray had called him? *An extra in an adults-only seasonal special.* Along with Eli's too-tight costume and his make-up smeared and smudged, Grey was forced to admit the loathsome Murray had been right. Grey forced himself to look away. *Just deal with the practicalities... Warm, dry clothes and something to eat and drink...* It would save Grey from having to think too closely about what the hell he was doing.

Grey had caught Colin's eye in the rear view mirror when he said he wanted to turn around and check on Eli. The driver's face had remained impassive as he'd obeyed the request without question, but the chauffeur hadn't approved, and had approved even less when Grey had offered Eli a bed for the night. Grey didn't give a damn what Colin thought, but he'd known the man long enough to know he'd keep his own counsel and the events of this evening would go no further. If they did, there were other chauffeur services Gillespie Associates could switch to.

"Er, yes. Thanks."

Eli's attention wasn't on Grey, but on the large square entrance hall, every inch lit with warm light from the huge modern, minimalist chandelier.

"I think the whole of Benny's house would fit into here, but yes please, to a change of clothes." Eli switched his focus to Grey. "This stupid costume was uncomfortable before, but now it's wet it's chaffing. Whoops, that was probably TMI." Eli smiled, but patches of red stained his cheeks.

Too much information? Probably, but the costume really did seem to have shrunk. The leggings were moulded around Eli's long legs, and the jacket hugged every inch of his willowy torso. Grey's stomach muscles tightened. Jesus, since when had sexy little elves been a thing—

Eli's exaggerated cough snagged Grey's attention. The younger man was staring at him, his heterochromatic eyes dazzling. Had Eli read his thoughts? His very inappropriate thoughts?

"The first thing I need to do, though, is cancel my debit card. With the bank. Not that there's much in the account, but..." Eli shrugged. "If I could, erm, use your phone?"

"Yes, of course. And your mobile, you'll need to get in touch with your network provider. And what about your keys?"

Eli shook his head. "The phone was a piece of crap

pay-as-you-go that was on its last legs with less than £10.00 credit left on it. Whoever was mad enough to steal it has probably chucked it away in disgust. As for the keys, there was nothing with them that identifies the house. It's just my bank card I need to sort out."

"Who do you bank with?"

Eli told him and Grey pulled up the website before handing the phone over, earning himself a smile before Eli turned aside.

"All done," Eli said a couple of minutes later. "They've frozen the card, and are sending me a replacement." Eli handed back the phone, his fingers brushing against Grey's.

"Good. Follow me." Grey led the way upstairs, his fingers tingling and his voice gruffer than he'd intended. Behind him, Eli jingled with every step. "There's an en-suite if you want a shower, with plenty of toiletries and a spare toothbrush. I'll find you something to put on. It'll be too big but—"

"Anything will do. Seriously, it doesn't matter. Well, not another nylon elf costume, perhaps, but then I don't imagine you've got too many of those hanging in your wardrobe? Or…?"

Grey laughed, and Eli joined in.

"No elf costumes, I promise. I'll see what I can find, and I'll leave it on the end of the bed. Come downstairs when you're ready, to the kitchen."

"Cute doggie. Part dachshund?"

"Yes, that's right." Grey swung around. His mouth

dried and his pulse spiked, because it wasn't only the tiny mutt playing around his feet that was cute.

Eli smiled at him as he folded the arms back on the sweatshirt Grey had left for him. The navy top and the matching tracksuit bottoms swamped Eli, but anything Grey owned would do so because although Eli was probably around five foot ten, Grey was a good six inches or so taller, and broader to match.

With his face washed clean of the make-up he'd been forced to wear, Grey could see how pale Eli was, emphasised by the first faint shadow of dark scruff. Eli was stunning, no two ways, and for one shocking and blinding moment, Grey understood why Murray had dragged Eli onto his lap.

What the—?

No. There was nothing to understand about it, nothing at all, yet Grey couldn't control or deny the frisson that skittered down his spine. Forcing the exciting, disturbing thought away, Grey managed, just, to switch to his cool and logical head, the one that had made him wealthy and had cemented his place in the hard, unforgiving world of finance.

He looks so tired and worn out.

The muscles in Grey's stomach twisted and tightened as he studied the faint shadows staining the skin beneath Eli's eyes; he looked as though he'd not slept properly in days, or weeks. Grey swallowed. He understood not sleeping, staring up at the ceiling and watching the sunrise creep its way across.

What keeps you staring at the ceiling, Eli? What keeps you awake at night?

Eli had stopped folding back the overlong sleeves, and

was looking at the pan on the hob and the bowl set out next to it, along with the bread.

"I thought you might like some soup. Other than the basics, I'm out of almost everything until my grocery delivery arrives."

Eli's face lit up in a bright smile, disguising for a moment how exhausted he looked.

"Soup's great. I've not had anything to eat since breakfast. I was expecting to eat after the party, but we know how that turned out." The brightness in his face dimmed as he settled himself at the table. "Who's your girlfriend? Is it a she? Can't see from here." Eli peered at the dog, who retreated around the central island, its long snout peeking out from around the corner.

"She's a he. No girlfriend for me." Grey glanced at Eli, holding his gaze for a beat as he put the soup in front of Eli. "He's called Trevor."

Eli's hand, clutching the soup spoon, stopped part way between the bowl and his mouth.

"Trevor. You called your cute little dog *Trevor*? What did he do to warrant such a heinous punishment?"

Grey shrugged. "It seemed to suit him." It hadn't been his choice, but Eli didn't need to know that. "It's too late to change it now, because it's what he answers to. And anyway, it could have been worse. He could have been called Kestrel."

Eli huffed. "Touché. I have no idea why I told you my middle name. I never tell anybody." Eli's brows scrunched together as though the admission was a revelation not only to Grey but to himself, too.

A young man with a laughable middle name bequeathed him by hippy parents, a man who Grey reckoned must be a good twenty years younger, if not more, than his own forty-three, and who'd come into his life dressed as an elf... *What's your story, Eli?* With a longing that grabbed at him, Grey wanted to know more about the boy who sat in his kitchen. Instead, he let Eli get on with the soup as he pretended to make himself busy, wiping down surfaces his cleaner had left pristine and sparkling.

"That was great, thank you."

Grey looked across as Eli bent down from the waist, his hand outstretched towards Trevor. The little dog was nervy, and looked between Grey and Eli, indecision in his big brown eyes. Grey opened his mouth, about to tell Eli attempting to coax Trevor over to him was a lost cause, but his eyes widened as the dog made his careful way across the kitchen and sniffed Eli's proffered hand.

"What are you when you're not being an elf? A dog whisperer?"

"I grew up with dogs, and various other animals. As for being an elf, that particular career path is now closed to me. But I'm not sorry about what I did to that creep, although it does mean I've lost out on a good booking for New Year's Eve with Jolly Eventful. You're a handsome boy, aren't you Trevor?" Eli cooed, as he gently stroked Trevor's smooth fur. "Disco Divas."

"Excuse me?"

Eli tilted his head and grinned as he looked up at Grey.

Impish. The word fizzed in Grey's head. Or maybe elfish. Or maybe not.

"Disco Divas, the theme of the party I'm now not working. Along with all the other waiting staff, I was going to be dressed up in gold hot pants, with a wig to represent a

40

well known diva. Cher, Diana Ross, and such like. Oh, and this was the piece of brilliance Jolly Eventful particularly prided itself on." Eli sat upright as Trevor wandered back to his cushion in the corner of the kitchen. "We'd all be on roller skates as we whizzed around with trays of drinks."

Grey wrinkled his nose. "That sounds horrible." Except for the gold hot pants.

"Yep, but the decidedly *unjolly* Ms. Sheena Jolly was paying over the odds for specialist skills — a.k.a. balancing a tray of lurid cocktails whilst swishing around on skates. Everybody had to audition for the privilege. It was like one of those cyclist proficiency tests, where you wobble and weave around traffic cones. I passed because I'm a red hot roller skater. The whole thing was a fiasco, but by the end of it as long as you remained upright you got the job. Most couldn't. One girl broke her ankle. That old bag Sheena didn't think about that when she binned me off tonight. I'll take great delight in telling her where to stick her diva wig and roller skates when she calls, begging me to come back. Or I would, but my phone's been nicked. Except I wouldn't tell her any of that, because I need the money seeing that dreams don't come free." Eli yawned. "Sorry. It's just that it's been a long and eventful day." He snorted. "Yeah, eventful and anything but jolly."

"Yes, yes of course." Grey threw aside the cloth he'd stopped pretending to use. "Go up if you want. As you say, you've had a day of it."

Eli pushed his chair back. "I will. Goodnight. And goodnight to you too, Trevor." He smiled over at the dog, curled up in the corner. "And thank you." Eli looked back at Grey. "If you hadn't have come back, I'd have been stuck. Or arrested, given my luck today."

"Sleep well."

"I fully intend to." With a quick smile, Eli was gone.

Grey pulled a bottle of scotch from the back of one of the cupboards. Pouring himself a drink, he nursed the tumbler between his hands. As he cradled his drink, Grey wondered what those dreams of Eli's were, and whether or not he'd get the chance to find out.

CHAPTER SEVEN

"Oh, shit."

Holding aside the heavy curtain, Eli stared out over the huge garden, blanketed by a thick layer of snow.

As soon as his head had hit the soft pillow, he'd fallen into a deep and dreamless sleep, the best he'd had in ages, but with morning had come a cruel reminder that his position hadn't changed from last night. Letting Grey persuade him to come back with him had only delayed what he had to do, which was to get back into the house. It also meant putting that bloody horrible elf suit back on. Perhaps Grey would let him keep the clothes he'd leant him, just for now?

Eli let the curtain fall back as a soft knock sounded at the door.

"Come in."

Grey stood in the doorway, and Eli's stomach did a somersault. Christ, Grey had looked good last night, all expensive sharp suit, shiny shoes, and perfectly knotted tie. Corporate and buttoned up, not a hair out of place, the guy had been pure suit porn — but Eli liked the version of Grey who now stood before him just as much.

Dark jeans, which sat on him just right, and a torso hugging T-shirt in the same dark blue shade as his eyes. With the hand that wasn't glued to the door knob, Grey pushed his fallen forward dark blond hair from his brow, making it stick up. Yes, Eli liked this version of Grey; it was a definite case of *This* or *That,* and Eli was stumped over which to pick.

"I hope you slept well?"

"I did. Thank you."

"Good."

Grey kept his hand on the door knob as Eli tucked his hair, damp from the shower he'd luxuriated in, back behind his ears. It was getting long, but a haircut was the least of his worries at the moment. The silence was stretching out, and Eli leapt in to fill it. Grey beat him to it.

"There's breakfast downstairs. It's a bit cobbled together, I'm afraid, but at least there's plenty of coffee. When you're ready." Grey dashed off before Eli could answer.

Eli made his way downstairs, his nose twitching as his stomach gurgled. Was that bacon he could smell? His mouth began to water at the treat, so different from the budget brand cornflakes that didn't stretch his finances too much.

The kitchen table was set with two places, opposite each other. In between was a plate piled with toast and a dish of butter.

"Bacon and eggs okay? Sorry, I should have checked to see if you were veggie, or anything?" Grey lifted the frying pan from the hob, an unsure look flitting across his face.

"No, I'm not. And I'd hardly call bacon, egg, and toast as being cobbled together. I thought you didn't have anything in?" Realisation dawned on Eli as Grey answered with a sheepish grin. "Did you go out to the shops? You didn't need to, not for me." *But I'm glad you did...* Warmth fluttered through Eli's belly, and he smiled.

"I had to take Trevor out for his walk, even though I ended up carrying him most of the way, so I killed two birds with one stone. And in this weather you're going to need something hot to eat."

"Yes, I suppose I will. Thank you." Eli kept his smile in place by force of will alone. Grey's words were a stark reminder his welcome in Grey's house would last only so long. *He'll let me keep the stuff he leant me, just for now, won't he...?*

Grey made them both coffee from the shiny all-singing, all-dancing coffee maker before he served up and they tucked into their breakfast. For a few glorious minutes, every shitty thing that had happened to Eli was wiped from his memory as he gave every ounce of concentration to the food. Hot salty bacon, crisp and singed at the edges, and buttery scrambled eggs, all accompanied by crunchy, chewy sourdough toast. It was enough to make an angel weep.

"That was fantastic." Eli pushed his knife and fork together and sat back with a sigh. "Benny, my landlord and supposed friend, won't have meat in the house because of Lenny. Before Lenny, Benny all but lived on supermarket economy burgers and sausages."

"Sorry — but Benny and *Lenny*?"

"Yeah, they sound like an old time comedy duo, don't they? Except, since Lenny's been on the scene, things haven't exactly been a barrel of laughs. Or at least, not for me. But I'm going to be moving out soon."

"Ah, I see. Or at least I think I do. Two's company but three's a crowd?" Across the table from him, Grey raised a questioning brow. A nicely groomed brow, but not too groomed…

Eli cleared his throat. "Got it in one. Things were fine until Lenny moved in, and he made it plain from the beginning there wasn't room for me."

"Any other friends you could share with?"

Grey gathered up the plates, and held up his mug to ask if more coffee was wanted. Eli nodded his thanks.

"Not immediately, which means I'm going to have to grit my teeth and sit tight for a little while, even if it does hack them off. Most of my friends are kind of in the same position as good ol' Ben and Len — loved up, and not looking for a third. I mean a lodger—"

Grey laughed, a low, deep rumbly sound that sent a low, deep rumble all the way down into Eli's groin. His dick twitched. *God no, not now…* Eli shifted in his seat, and tugged the long sweatshirt lower.

"I know what you mean. But you said *not immediately*, which implies there is somebody who can help you out, if not quite yet." Grey raised his brows in question.

"There's Rufus, a friend of mine. Trouble is, his place is currently rented out as he's working abroad and he won't be returning until the end of February. I'll be able to rent a room at his place, but it's just outside London and nowhere near a tube station. Or any station, which is okay if you have a car. Which I don't." Eli shrugged. Despite his friend living in the back and beyond, if he could just hang on at Benny's for now—

"…your parents?"

"Hmm? What?" Eli blinked up at Grey. "Oh, yes. Sorry. Isolated little rock of a Scottish island, remember? All that fresh air would kill me. And way too remote. I thrive on diesel fumes, traffic clogged streets and urban edge. Seriously, where they are is beautiful, but it wouldn't work, even for a little while. I just hope I'm not forced to put it to the test."

Eli bit his thumb nail, gnawing away at it as worry gnawed at this stomach. His parents, much as he loved them, were the very last resort. What he wanted to do, he couldn't do on the tiny rock of an island.

"Why wouldn't it—?" But Grey didn't get any further as his mobile rang, cutting across the question. He pulled his phone from his pocket and frowned at the screen. "Sorry, it's work. I need to take this."

Eli watched as Grey left the kitchen, unsure whether or not he wanted to answer Grey's question. He still had some way to go before he could make his ambition a reality, and until then he wanted to hold it close. His shoulders sagged. Finding someplace new to live was an expense he could do without, as he'd have no choice but to dig into his carefully harvested savings. Why was his life always one step forward, and ten back?

A tap of claws on the tiled floor was accompanied by a bark that was far too loud for Trevor's tiny size.

"Hey, you." Eli scooped the dog up. Depositing him on his lap, he tickled him behind one of his floppy brown ears. "You don't fool me, it's because you can smell the bacon. Greedy sausage!" Trevor squirmed on Eli's lap as he tried to lap Eli's nose with his tongue. "Oh no you don't, didn't I tell you I don't kiss on first dates?"

"Oh!"

Eli looked up. Grey stood in the doorway, surprise etched on his face.

"Me and Trevor are just getting better acquainted."

"That's the second time he's surprised me in less than twelve hours. He's normally nervy and doesn't much like anybody handling him except me."

Eli put Trevor down, his face heating and throbbing at the thought of being handled by Grey, but the ping of an oversized wall clock, marking the morning's eleventh hour, was all the reminder he didn't want that it was time for him to leave. He stood up.

"Look, I know this is probably a bit cheeky, but can I keep these for now? Until I get back into the house? I'll, erm, need a pair of shoes of some kind." Eli looked down at his bare feet, where his toes were curling with embarrassment. "And the lend of some money so I can get the tube back to Stockwell. Please."

Grey said nothing as he stared at him from across the kitchen. His face was still and expressionless, his dark blue eyes opaque and unreadable. Whatever was going on behind their inky depths, it was impossible to know. Eli wanted to squirm and turn away. Maybe he was asking too much, but what choice did he have? He forced himself to hold Grey's stare.

"I can do as you ask." Grey's brow creased, shattering his unnerving icy stillness, as he walked into the kitchen and propped himself on the edge of the table. Eli let go of a silent, and relieved, long breath. "But how would it help you?"

It was Eli's turn to frown. "I need to get back, and into the house, even if I've got to try and break in to do it. I've got no option. And I'd rather not try and make the journey back in my elf costume."

The horrible bloody thing really had shrunk. He'd placed it over the radiator in the en-suite, where the heat had wrinkled and shrunk the tights, and the jacket had gone crinkly. Now, the outfit might just about fit a ten-year-old. A very small ten-year-old.

"Breaking and entering, in other words. If that's not enough to get you arrested, being seen in public dressed in that elf costume most certainly is."

Eli blinked. Then what the hell was he supposed…? He groaned, and rolled his eyes.

Grey's lips lifted in a crooked smile. "I'm sorry, I don't mean to make light of your situation but I do have a possible temporary solution. Sit down, hear me out, and then make your decision."

Eli flopped back down into the chair. "A possible solution? There's only one as far as I can see, and it's the same as yesterday's."

"There's always more than one option. Stay here, until Benny gets back. I've got more than enough room. Why risk arrest when you don't have to? If you're caught, you'll end up with a criminal record. Do you really want that?"

"But… I…"

Eli's words stumbled from his lips, too stunned by Grey's proposition. And as for risking arrest, the way his luck had been going it was a foregone certainty, which could dog him and scupper all his closely held ambitions… It was the perfect short term solution to his situation, but Eli knew enough of life to know nothing was ever perfect, and conditions were often attached.

"Why are you asking me to stay? You helped me out last night, and I'm so, so grateful. But you don't really know me. And I don't know you." Eli swallowed as Grey gave him his impenetrable stare that made Eli want to whimper and dip his head like a cowed dog.

"What you really want to know, is do I have an ulterior motive for asking you to stay? Beyond feeling in some small way I've been a factor in your current predicament, then no."

"I've told you, it's not your fault prune face sacked me."

"No, but it was my employee, a representative of my firm, that led to that happening. So yes, I do feel a responsibility, and that's not going to change."

Eli licked his lips, and looked down the long kitchen towards the wall of glass at the end that looked out over the same garden he'd gazed out on earlier, when his heart had plummeted. It was still snowing, the flakes adding layer upon layer. The weather forecasters had predicted at least a foot of snow in London, but it had gone way beyond that. There would be travel chaos, the buses, tube, and trains screwed up. Getting across London, back to a house he was locked out of, felt as impossible as travelling to the moon. He'd stayed last night, so what was so wrong with staying for a few more…?

The tap of claws on the floor was followed by a sharp yap, as Trevor wobbled up on his stubby back legs. Eli whisked him up and the small dog snuggled into his lap, his warm and furry body a comforting weight. Eli looked up at Grey.

"Yes, I will stay, and thank you. But it's only because you have the cutest little kind of sausage dog. I would be doing it for Trevor."

Grey nodded, his expression grave and serious. "Of course, that's fully understood. He's very attractive and hard to resist."

Eli nodded. Trevor wasn't the only man in the house who was attractive and irresistible. He rubbed his face into the dog's short fur to hide the smile that spread across his face.

"Eli?"

Eli looked up and met Grey's steady gaze.

"I just want to be clear about something, should you be wondering. Be assured you'll be safe here. There are no conditions of any kind attached to my offer. Of *any* kind." Grey pulled his mobile from the pocket of his jeans, and punched in a code. "I want you to call your parents, to let them know where you are and for them to have my number." He put it on the table and pushed it across.

Eli blinked down at Grey's mobile. He hadn't, for one moment, believed he was anything other than safe with Grey. The man's care and concern was a warm and fuzzy blanket, one Eli wanted to wrap around himself and snuggle down into.

"Thank you," Eli croaked. "For everything."

Grey nodded, leaving the kitchen as Eli picked up the phone to make his call.

CHAPTER EIGHT

Grey rubbed his palms over his face before leaning forward and staring at himself in the bathroom mirror.

Had he lost his mind? It was the only reason he could think of for his rash offer. He owed Eli some help for what had happened last night, but beyond that? The boy wasn't his to look out for. The sensible thing, after he'd dropped Eli back last night, would have been to have driven away and not turned back. Grey huffed, because it hadn't taken much more than one look at Eli and any thoughts about *the sensible thing* had been wiped from his brain.

Eli had looked so wretched, hunkered down and hiding in the footwell of the car, stirring up that ever present need which lay at the core of who Grey was. The need to protect, to care for, to keep safe, all of it had rushed to the surface as unstoppable as white hot lava erupting from a long dormant volcano. None of those needs, as much a part of him as breathing, would have been appeased if he'd had Colin continue to drive him home. So he'd done what he'd done, telling himself it had been the right thing to do, when it had been so much more.

Grey turned the cold tap on full. He doused his face in the icy water and, taking a deep breath, made his way back downstairs. He stood outside the closed kitchen door for a moment, listening for Eli's voice, but hearing nothing he opened up and went inside.

"Did you get through okay? To your parents?"

Eli nodded. "Eventually. It took a few tries and the reception was really bad. They asked me to thank you. Mum said she'd light a candle for you, and place it on the altar at sunset. Or at least I think that's what she said, but knowing Mum, that sounds about right."

"Your parents are Roman Catholics?"

Eli burst out laughing, and Trevor, still curled up on Eli's lap, yapped and jumped down, skittering away to his pillow.

"No. Aged hippies, remember? She's got a shrine in the garden, to some goddess. Load of old boll—erm, old tut," he muttered, as he pushed the long sleeves of his borrowed sweatshirt up his arms; almost immediately they slipped down to his wrists.

Grey's brows knitted together. He'd offered Eli a place to stay until Benny got back in the New Year. That was over a week away. There was no way Eli could keep wearing borrowed clothes that came nowhere near close to fitting him. He took a breath. *In for a penny, in for a pound.*

"You need some other clothes to wear whilst you're staying here. Some jeans and jumpers, and so on. The usual kind of thing. I think we should sort that out."

"Oh." Eli looked down at himself. "I never thought

about that. I suppose so. I can't get the elf costume back on, even if I wanted to." He looked up, red patches colouring his cheeks. "Look, are you sure you've thought this through? Me staying here, that is? I seem to be causing more trouble than I'm worth."

Something in Eli's voice, so tiny most wouldn't have noticed it. But Grey noticed. More trouble than Eli was worth? There it was, that vulnerability again, so well hidden beneath his bright and breezy manner.

"You're not causing me any trouble. And in answer to your question, yes, I have thought it through." *Liar.*

"S'pose you're right. I can't keep wearing your clothes." Eli offered up a sheepish smile. "I can ask my parents to reimburse you, straight away. They might be a couple of hippies but even they're not immune to internet banking. If the internet's working that is, which it often isn't. That's the price of living on a rock in the Atlantic."

"We can sort that out later." Grey had no intention of being paid back. What was the price of a few items of clothing? He had more money than he knew what to do with, and nobody to spend it on. Or not anymore.

"Thank you. I'll need some footwear of some kind because I don't think elf shoes with bells on them are going to be much use."

Grey laughed. Eli had looked cute and a whole lot more in his elf costume, but he'd keep that nugget to himself.

"I'll sort you something, and then we'll head out. The weather's only going to deteriorate, so let's get it done with."

Less than twenty minutes later, Grey turned the ignition on in his Range Rover. The big four wheeled drive rumbled into life and they set off towards a nearby indoor shopping centre, the car gliding along the road taking the snow and ice in its stride. Grey glanced at Eli, next to him, and suppressed a smile. Eli was bundled up in an old coat, which reached almost to his ankles. The boots Grey had found for him were at least three sizes too big, and he'd had to give Eli another pair of socks to help pad them out.

They didn't say much on the journey, as Grey concentrated on driving in the treacherous conditions, but the long silences didn't feel awkward and there was no need to fill them with meaningless chat. Grey turned into the shopping centre car park, the place nowhere near as busy as he'd expected.

"The weather must be keeping people away," Eli said, voicing Grey's own thoughts.

They climbed out but Eli had taken no more than a couple of steps when his feet went from under him and he landed with a howling yelp. Spreadeagled on his back, his face was white with shock.

"Eli? Eli, are you okay? Have you injured yourself?"

Eli sat up. "My bum took the brunt of it. I'm just winded. It all looked worse than it was."

Grey helped him to his feet, not believing a word Eli said, as he wrapped his arm tightly around him to hold him steady.

"I'll be okay," Eli muttered.

"Lean against me, I'll take your weight. The first thing we'll do is get you something sweet to eat and drink. For the shock."

"Yes, Daddy."

Grey jolted.

Daddy...

Eli's breathed out word, accompanied by a soft chuckle, sent an electrified shiver all the way through to Grey's groin.

"But I think a sit down might help. That and a cake." Eli looked up him, a wobbly smile on his lips.

"Come on, let me look after you," Grey said, his voice rough and croaky.

"Seem to be needing a lot of looking after at the moment."

"Just accept it."

Eli leaned into Grey. Warm embers glowed bright deep in Grey's chest, as with his arm tight around Eli, they made their steady way inside.

Like the car park, the shopping centre was a lot less busy than it should have been this close to Christmas, and they easily found a table in a ground floor café.

Making sure Eli was as comfortable as he could be, Grey queued at the counter, all the time keeping an eye on Eli.

Hunched over the table, wrapped up in Grey's coat, Eli looked like a kid dressed in his big brother's hand-me-downs. *He looks so tired…* But it was more than tiredness, more than a few sleepless nights. Eli looked ground down by life. Grey's stomach clenched. Eli was far too young for the kicks and punches life so casually doled out. The desire, the need, to care for was a wave Grey couldn't resist. His breath caught hard in his chest. The need to…

Smother, and control.

The words burned through him, the words that had been thrown in his face months and months before. Not care for, not protect, not to cherish, but to *smother and control*. Grey shoved his fingers through his hair.

56

"What? Sorry?"

The young woman behind the counter was looking at him. "What would you like?"

"Sorry, miles away," he said with a smile, softening the woman's harassed expression.

A couple of minutes later, Grey set the laden tray down in front of Eli.

"Wow. Hot chocolate with marshmallows. And chocolate fudge cake, too. And what's this?" Eli looked closer at one of the plates. "Chocolate caramel cheesecake. Looks lovely, all of it. Shame I don't like chocolate."

Grey started. "You don't—?"

Eli chuckled. "I don't *like* it, I *love* it."

Grey rolled his eyes. "The sugar should help with the shock, or that's what I was always led to believe, even though it might rot your teeth and send you spiralling towards diabetes. Which would you like?" Grey nodded towards the two cakes.

"I get to choose between rotten teeth and diabetes? You spoil me."

Grey stared at Eli's deadpan expression before he let his head fall back as he laughed, causing nearby customers to turn his way.

Eli grinned. "We can share. Half and half?"

They divided the cakes between them and Eli forked a lump of the gooey chocolate cake into his mouth.

"Ohhhh." Eli closed his eyes and slumped back into his chair. "I think this is the best thing I've ever tasted. Or maybe the second best." His eyes snapped open, their opposing colours all but obscured by their black pupils.

Grey's pulse sped up and his dick filled and pulsed. The chatter in the café faded, replaced by the hard thud of

Grey's heart and the whoosh of blood through his veins. He couldn't move, he could hardly breath, as all he could do was stare.

Eli blinked and shifted in his seat, breaking through Grey's paralysis. Redness washed over Eli's face and he bent forward and gave all his attention to the cake. The sound of the crowd rushed back in, and Grey forced himself to look away, to his own food and drink, wondering for the smallest of seconds what they were and how they'd got there.

"Better?" Grey asked after a minute or two, when he'd taken a few surreptitious deep breaths and got his heart rate, along with his errant dick, back under control.

"Yes, much better thanks. They should prescribe chocolate on the NHS. A bone fide cure for shock. Hmm, lovely. It reminds me of my grandpa. He always used to make me hot chocolate with either cream or marshmallows if I wasn't feeling well when I was little. Mum and Dad didn't approve, and they always tried to get him to use some kind of chocolate alternative crap, but he wouldn't *have any of that dippy hippy old shit*, he'd say — he might have looked like everybody's cuddly old grandpa, but he used to swear like a trooper and didn't give a sod who heard him. He was great." Eli gave a soft smile. "He always encouraged me. '*Do what you want to do, lad, don't go listening to all those fuckers who try and make you do what* they *want you to do. Fuck the lot of 'em!*'" Eli laughed, and covered his mouth with the back of his hand. "That's what he used to say, word for word. He said it so many times, it's engraved on my heart."

Soon after, with nothing left other than empty mugs and crumb strewn plates, they set off from the café.

"Sure you're okay?" Grey asked, instinctively resting his palm on the small of Eli's back, whipping it away almost the moment it landed. Helping Eli to his feet, holding him when he stood on shaky legs was one thing, but—

"I am, thanks to you." Eli smiled up at him, but almost immediately it was replaced with a serious, worried frown. "Just a few things, okay? Just to tide me over, remember? I'm going to be gone before you know it, and I've got plenty of stuff at the house."

Grey pushed down the disappointment swelling inside him. But Eli was right, he'd soon be gone and out of his life as though he'd never been. He forced himself to smile.

"Jeans, jumpers, underwear, socks, shoes — or boots, for this weather — a coat of some kind, gloves, scarf..." Grey ticked the items off on his fingers, one by one.

"That much?" Eli bit down on his lower lip as his frown deepened, and Grey had to force his hands to stay still to not ease it away. "You're right, I suppose. But no coat."

"It's the middle of winter. It's snowing. Of course you're going to need a coat."

Eli shook his head, determination written across his face.

"Your old coat's fine — it's like being wrapped up in a big blanket. The other stuff I get, but I won't be wearing a coat in a warm house, will I?"

Grey huffed. He'd let Eli win this argument. "Let's get you sorted out with the rest of it. Okay?"

Eli hesitated, then nodded.

The crowds in the shopping centre had increased

during the time they'd been in the café, and the place thronged with frantic shoppers shoving this way and that.

"We should be able to get everything you need in here." Grey directed Eli into a large department store, and steered him towards the menswear department.

Eli halted in front of a large, full length mirror, pulling Grey to a stop, and grinned. "We're an odd looking couple, don't you think? I look like I'm playing dress up and—"

"Can I help you, gentlemen?" An assistant appeared and looked between them, his bland professional smile in place, but it couldn't disguise that he, too, thought they were indeed an unlikely looking pair.

The assistant could think what he bloody well wanted, because as far as Grey was concerned he and Eli looked just right. Grey fought the urge to growl at the assistant, and forced his voice to stay calm and level.

"My friend needs kitting out…"

It wasn't long before they'd found most of what they needed. Eli, weighed down by a large pile of clothes Grey had made sure was more than the *few things* Eli had insisted upon, made his way into the changing rooms as Grey lounged in a chair outside.

Grey closed his eyes and let the Christmas music playing in the background wash over him.

"What do you think?"

Grey jerked out of the fuzzy place between sleep and wakefulness he'd drifted into.

Hovering in the doorway to the changing room, Eli shuffled from foot to foot.

"The grey one, or the green?"

Eli wore a soft looking slate grey jumper. He peeled it off, pulling up the white T-shirt he wore underneath to reveal a flash of pale skin stretched tight over firm abdominal muscles, before he tugged on the other jumper. The grey or the green, jumpers Grey had picked out and insisted Eli take into the changing room, each the same shade as Eli's incredible, captivating eyes.

Eli looked good, more than good, in both. He'd look good in a paper bag, but in the tight dark jeans, which hugged him from ankles to hips, and in the fine wool jumper that fitted like a second skin, Eli was breathtaking.

"Grey? Which one? Or are they both horrible?" Eli looked down at himself.

"No! They're great. Either one, because both match your eyes."

Eli jerked his head up. "Good thing about heterochondria, I have more colour choices. But I still don't know."

"Both."

Eli's eyes widened a fraction, and he shook his head. "Just a few things, remember?"

"Both, because they're buy one get one half price. Haven't you seen the promotional signs all over the place?"

"Oh." Eli grinned. "Well, both it is then. Do you think they'll let me wear all this now, or do we have to pay first?"

"Wear it now." Grey didn't want to see those long, slim legs disappear under tracksuit bottoms that had to be turned up several times at the ankle cuff.

Eli darted back into the changing room, and came out laden down with the rest of the new clothes, along with those Grey had lent him.

"Wait." Grey stopped by a display on the way to the till, a fine, soft looking emerald green scarf catching his attention. It was perfect, and made for Eli. "You can't not have this."

"It's lovely — and oh my god, so's the price. It costs as much as the boots. And jeans. And maybe the jumpers, too. All combined."

"It's a Christmas present."

"No." Eli shook his head, stubbornness in every inch of his movement. "You've done — are doing — so much for me when you didn't have to do a thing. Honestly, that's the best Christmas present I could have."

"Well, the best present I could have is for you to accept. Really. Please, I'd like you to have it."

Eli ran his fingers across the scarf. "It *is* gorgeous…"

Grey snatched the advantage. He'd sent out so many gifts this Christmas season, all on his corporate credit card, selected by and purchased on his behalf by his PA. The only thing he'd done was give the final approval, and then every single item had been forgotten. This was the only gift he'd chosen himself, and it was perfect.

With the scarf carefully folded and wrapped in tissue paper, and added to the rest of the purchases, they made their way out of the department store. Frantic crowds of harassed shoppers pushed and shoved and tinny, jangling Christmas music blasted out from loud speakers.

"Time to go?" Grey asked, relieved when Eli nodded.

They made their way across the car park, Eli picking his way carefully as Grey kept a close watch on him, ready to jump if Eli looked like he was going to slip, but they got back to the car with no mishaps. It wasn't even three o'clock but already darkness was falling all around them.

Grey pulled his seatbelt on, and turned to Eli. "We can

stop off and pick up some pizzas, if you like? My grocery delivery doesn't come until tomorrow, so…"

"I love pizza. Well, I just love food."

Grey tamped down on a grin. Eli had certainly demolished breakfast and then the huge slab of cake, but slim and lithe, there wasn't an ounce of fat on him.

"That's settled, then. There's an excellent place just minutes from home."

"Or…" Eli's brow scrunched as he chewed on his lower lip. "We could get some good ready made bases and construct our own toppings. I'd make the bases, normally, but it'd take too long and I'm kind of guessing you don't stock yeast and strong bread or 0 grade flour in your kitchen cupboards?"

"Hmm, they're not generally on my grocery order. Sounds good, but do you want to go to all that trouble? I'm not great in the kitchen so I wouldn't be much use. I appreciate the idea, but you've had a fall, don't forget." The last thing Eli needed was to stand around cooking, when he should be taking it easy, and tucked up with a heap of pillows on the sofa.

"Yes, I fell on my bum but I didn't break any bones. I don't need you to be of help, because I'll do it. I want to. Honestly. Think of it as a way of me saying thank you — even if you will need to buy the ingredients."

And there it was again, the soft flush of red on Eli's cheeks, the colour of embarrassment. Grey wanted to wash all evidence of it away.

"Only if you're sure, that you're not too tired…"

Eli glared at him. Grey knew when he was defeated. He might not like it, but he knew.

"All right, and I have to admit it'll be a welcome

change to have somebody cook a meal for me. Bacon and eggs is about my limit, so I tend to order in when I'm not eating out." It was Grey's turn to feel the sting of embarrassment. He could do a little more than put a cooked breakfast together, but not a lot. Home cooked meals, like so many other things, belonged to the past. "We'll stop off for the supplies you need on the way home."

Eli answered with a wide grin which Grey couldn't fail but return. Moments later they were gliding out of the car park and were on their way.

CHAPTER NINE

Eli turned on the oven, and cranked it up as hot as it would go, then spread the ingredients for the toppings over the kitchen island worktop. The bases were thin, the crust encircling the rims puffy and singed.

Grey had driven straight past the supermarket, and had instead called in at a tiny Italian deli, just a couple of streets away from the house. If Eli had died on the spot, he'd have gone to meet the big guy on a cloud a very happy man. Grey had laughed when Eli had taken a step across the threshold, stood still and just — sniffed. The rich savoury aroma had made his mouth water and, as much as the place had smelled fantastic, it'd looked even better.

Premium Italian products had been stacked high, and overflowed from shelves. Behind the counter, hams and cheeses jostled for space with olives, tomatoes, and arti-chokes steeped in aromatic olive oil. And sweet treats, so many sweet treats. Cannoli, tiramisu, cantuccini, and everywhere, boxed-up panettone, looking like the perfect Christmas gift.

Grey had given him free range to choose what he wanted. The shopkeeper had offered advice, but Eli had politely declined. He'd known exactly what he wanted, even if his eclectic choice of purchases had provoked a very slight raise of the shopkeeper's brow.

Eli removed the lid from the tub of fresh tomato sauce he'd use for the base, and sighed as he took a long, appreciative sniff. He'd have loved to have made his own, but a good base sauce took time, which they didn't have. Next came the pears, ripe and juicy even in the midst of winter, which he cored and thinly sliced. Eli lost himself in the prep, contentment and ease rippling through his muscles which more often than not, recently, had been held tight and tense. The mounting problems of sharing with Benny and Lenny; the day job he was holding onto by a shoe string; the event work which was either cringe-inducing or downright humiliating, but which paid well — or had done until #ElfGate — all of it faded to nothing as he spread and sliced and chopped.

A bottle clunked down next to him, and he jumped.

"You're miles away." Grey wrapped his lips around the top of his own bottled beer, his eyes narrowing and trained on Eli as he tipped his head back and gulped.

Eli's chest tightened, his throat constricted, and his mouth dried to dust. He grabbed up the bottle, his eyes watering as he forced a mouthful of the light, citrusy lager past the lump in his throat.

"Yeah," he croaked, dragging his gaze away from Grey and back to the ingredients littering the work surface. "Cooking tends to make me go that way." He blinked at the lined-up elements of the pizza he wanted to wow Grey with, but just now the wowing was definitely on the other foot.

Grey pulled a stool up and sat down at the end of the huge island. Eli glanced across as Grey's legs fell apart slightly as he hooked his feet around the metal legs of the stool. The kitchen was warm, and Grey had peeled his jumper off, leaving just his T-shirt to hug his broad, built torso.

Stop it, just stop it…

Grey was helping him out of a very awkward patch, and things would get a lot more awkward for him if Grey caught him looking at, staring, ogling, salivating over his body that was way more mouthwatering than the pizza he needed to concentrate on.

"Pear? On a pizza? I thought the pear was maybe for afters."

Eli swallowed. A pear wasn't his idea of *afters*. He shoved the dangerous thought aside.

"It works," Eli said, his voice way groggier than it should have been. "Just have faith in me. Pear on pizza…"

The rest of Eli's words died, and it took every ounce of effort to push down on the whimper that fought to escape his throat as Grey leaned across and snagged a piece of the thinly sliced fruit, its juice running down his fingers which he sucked clean, letting go of each digit with a wet smack.

Oh, fuck… Eli rearranged the long white chef's apron, an apron belonging to a man who by his own admission hardly cooked, thankful it was loose and long enough to hide the sweetly painful bulge pushing out the front of his jeans. He shuffled in closer to the worktop, its edge pushed in against his stomach. Just to be safe, just to be sure.

"I do, as far as the pizza's concerned. I think. I always have the same thing. Cheese and tomato. A little unimaginative, I suppose."

Eli barked out a laugh, releasing the heat that had built up inside of him. "If it's what you like, and a good cheese and tomato is a wonderful thing, but I think you could use a bit more flavour in your life, don't you?"

"Yes, I think you're right." Grey's lips twisted into a smile, but there was no trace of humour, only sadness tinged with resignation. The laughter on Eli's lips faded. Grey looked away as he took a long draught of his lager. Whatever question Grey had been answering, it had nothing to do with pizza.

Eli busied himself with checking the oven temperature and quickly assembled the pizza, spreading the rich and tangy tomato sauce over the base, before scattering the sliced pears across the top and then finishing off with chunks — and plenty of them — of salty Gorgonzola cheese.

"This one's a bit more traditional," Eli said with a grin, as he repeated the process with the second base, adding oily sun blushed tomatoes from a small tub and finishing it with torn pieces of mozzarella before adding a generous drizzle of olive oil and salt and pepper.

"For my bland palette, you mean?" Grey raised his brows, as though challenging Eli to contradict him.

Eli titled his head. "There's nothing bland about you."

Grey's brows lifted higher, and Eli beat back the squirm that slithered to escape him. "What I mean is—"

"That my tastes run to the more traditional, hmm? Is that what you think?" Grey's lips lifted in a secret smile as his eyes narrowed.

"Erm…" Heat washed through Eli's face, and pulsed in his groin. He felt disorientated and wrong footed, as though there was something his head wasn't getting but his body was. Whatever they were talking about, he didn't think it had much to do with pizza toppings.

"But maybe I'm ready for something different." Grey got up and began to gather the tubs and bottles and packets littering the worktop. "I'll clear up and you get the pizzas in the oven."

Eli nodded, not trusting himself to speak.

Grey set plates and cutlery at the table, and a couple more bottled lagers appeared. Within minutes, the pizzas were ready and Eli got them out of the oven. Cutting them into generous sized slices, Eli placed them onto a large serving platter Grey had ready for him. Eli's stomach rumbled as he breathed in the rich savoury tang of the food. The cheese and tomato was ready to eat, but the other had two more ingredients to be added. Before heading to the table, Eli pulled out the additions from the shopping bag.

"Walnuts and honey? On a pizza?" Grey peered at the packet of plain nuts and the bottled honey as though they were alien beings which needed to be backed away from, and fast.

"They're what make this pizza special. Believe me."

Eli didn't give Grey a chance to say no, as he scattered pieces of walnut over the melted Gorgonzola-topped pizza and then drizzled the honey over it all.

"Salt and sweet, creamy and sharp. The perfect flavour combo."

At the table, Eli picked up a slice, ignoring the knife and fork Grey had set out, and bit into the pizza. He closed his eyes and hummed as the flavours burst on his tongue.

"Oh. My. God. Is this better than sex, or is this better than sex?" He moaned as he swallowed and took another mouthful.

Grey's tight cough dragged Eli's eyes open. Grey was bent over his plate, gingerly scraping the nuts and honey off the top of the pizza.

Oh... "Do you have a nut allergy? I'm sorry, I should have checked first."

"I'm only allergic to having nuts and honey on my pizza. I was pushing the boat out with pear, but—"

Eli all but lunged across the table, and plucked the knife and fork from Grey's hands.

"Thought you said you were ready for something different? And all the best pizzas should be eaten with your fingers."

Grey had made a mess of his pizza, with the top all but scraped clean. Eli grabbed a fresh slice, the cheesy, oozy tip drooping slightly. Grey's eyes flashed with horror as Eli held it just a hair's breadth from his lips.

"Try it. One bite, that's all I'm asking. It may not be like anything you've had before, but I promise you once you've had a taste..."

Eli's words dissolved like melted cheese. Grey was staring at him, his face expressionless but his eyes dark, intense lasers. For a moment, Eli faltered as indecision grasped at him. Had he taken too much of a liberty? Could his reaction be seen as aggressive? Would Grey push his hand aside, and shove the plate away? His hand began to shake and he made to pull back but Grey wrapped his palm around his wrist, steadying him.

A burning shock ran the length of Eli's arm. He didn't know if it was because of Grey's intense blue eyes burning into his own, the firm, sure grip on his wrist, or a combination of both. But one thing he did know, and that was that he was helpless to move, helpless almost to breathe, as Grey opened his mouth and with his gaze still locked to Eli's, leant forward and clamped his lips around the sweet-salty, luscious tip of the pizza.

Grey's eyes widened a fraction, then fluttered to a close. He bit down on the pizza; slowly, he began to chew. His grip on Eli's wrist relaxed, then dropped away, as he slumped back in his chair. He groaned in unabashed, unashamed pleasure. Eli still held out the pizza slice, which dropped from his trembling fingers and landed on the platter.

Grey opened his eyes. The sharp clear blue of his irises was fogged, or what could be seen of them because of the wide dilation of his pupils. A light flush washed over his cheeks, and his lips glistened from oil and honey. Grey swallowed and he dragged the back of one hand over his lips, his gaze never leaving Eli's.

He looks like he's been...

Fucked.

The thought seared Eli's brain as heat seared his body; his breath caught in his throat, hot and burning.

Grey's lips lifted in a lazy smile. "You said I needed to try something different."

"You said it first," Eli croaked, his mouth and throat rough and dry. "And do you like it?"

Grey nodded, the movement slow. "I do. It — it surprised me."

"In a good way?"

"In a very good way."

Grey's smile deepened, and Eli didn't care about anything other than its warmth as it caressed his skin like summer sun. His body still tingled and reverberated from Grey's confident, strong touch, and he craved to feel it over and over again. Eli placed his hands flat on the table, ready to push up, ready to forget about the pizzas he'd been hungry for just moments before. He was still hungry, still eager to taste and savour, but it wasn't food he wanted and needed. All he had to do was to stand and take Grey's warm, strong hand and—

A sharp, loud bark broke through the heady, heavy atmosphere. Trevor, his tail wagging, padded over to them and sat down, his head whipping between Eli and Grey.

"Sorry, Trevor, you're just going to have to wait. Human dinner comes before canine." Grey stared down at the dog. "I mean it, so don't look at me like that. Oh, for goodness sake, all right." Grey got up and pulled out a bag of dry food from a cupboard, and emptied some into Trevor's bowl, tucked in a far corner. The small dog danced around him, tail wagging, and barking with excitement.

Eli let out a long breath and closed his eyes for a second, pulling himself together and stepping back from the precipice he'd almost tumbled head first over.

Back at the table, Grey devoured the rest of the pizza slice. "You're right about this. I'd have never thought of these flavour combinations, but it's great. Thank you."

"Told you so." Eli took a swig of lager, too fast and too much, and it burned he back of his throat and made him wince.

Grey, digging into the pile of pizza, didn't notice. Eli

picked up a slice, oblivious as to which of the two types it was, and ate mechanically, hardly tasting a thing.

What the hell had he been about to do? But he knew. Every muscle, nerve and cell, every atom in his body had screamed for him to grab Grey by the hand and drag him upstairs — no, scrub that — to push him down on the table and kiss all that hot salty sweetness from Grey's lips. Kiss and a whole lot more. A second, a split second, a fucking nanosecond later, and he'd have done it.

Eli glanced over at Trevor, crunching his way through his food. *Thanks Trev, thanks a bundle...*

Yet maybe he did owe the little dog for his untimely appearance. What if he'd had made the move he'd come so close to, and Grey had rejected him? Eli's stomach clenched and his skin crawled with the cringing, imagined embarrassment of such a miscalculation. Even if Grey didn't ask him to leave, he'd have had no option but to go.

Eli put his hand out for another slice of pizza, the motion automatic, but the platter was empty except for a few crumbs and a smear of grease. He'd no idea how many slices he'd eaten. Opposite him, Grey smiled down at Trevor who, unnoticed by Eli, had returned, and now lay on his back exposing his belly for Grey's tickles.

The fringe of Grey's dark blond hair fell forward. His profile was strong and chiselled, and more than handsome enough to grace the pages of a men's style magazine. He looked relaxed and at ease, more so than Eli had seen before. If anything had happened, would that have still been the case? As he watched Grey play with Trevor, Eli didn't know if he was brave enough to put it to the test.

CHAPTER TEN

Alone in the kitchen, Grey leaned against the glass doors leading out to his snow-filled garden as he waited for the kettle to boil. Fat flakes tumbled from the sky, adding yet more inches to the already banked-up snow.

He was looking without seeing, because all that filled his head was Eli leaning into him, his soft mouth slightly open, the tip of his pink tongue stroking his damp lower lip. And his eyes... Grey's stomach clenched hard. One green, one smokey grey, they'd been blazing at him. Not that there had been much iris to be seen, as midnight dark pupils had devoured all their colour. Just as he'd wanted to devour Eli. It had taken all his strength, all his willpower, not to knock Eli's hand away and pull him up from the table and drag him upstairs to his bed.

Grey sucked in a long, slow breath as he closed his eyes and pressed his forehead against the glass. Want, need, and desire had consumed him, and he'd taken Eli's wrist not to steady the younger man's hand, but to steady himself.

Pouring water into the waiting mugs, Grey tried to concentrate on making the tea, but he was powerless to stop his thoughts returning to Eli, who was waiting for him in the living room.

"Don't even think about it," Grey muttered to himself as he gave one of the bags a vicious stab, sloshing tea over the side.

Eli was here, in his house, under his protection. Grey might not have lost him his job with the events company, but Eli had lost it due to one of Grey's employees. Or ex-employee. He owed Eli some form of recompense, but what he didn't owe him was some kind of proprietary advance. It would make him no better than that slimeball Murray.

But... Grey's hand slowed and then stopped. The way Eli had looked at him, eyes glazed, pupils blown, and that long slow sweep of his tongue... Eli had swallowed hard, and not just once, and his breath had picked up, almost to a pant. Grey swore he'd heard Eli's heart rate quicken. In those few seconds he'd known, with every jangling nerve in his body on high alert, that Eli had wanted him as much as he'd wanted Eli.

Yet... Grey stared down at the mugs. If he made a move, would Eli feel he had no choice but to respond because he had no other option? And what would Grey see in those breathtaking, heart stopping eyes? Regret, reproach? Powerlessness? Grey's stomach tightened, knotting his insides and making him wince. No, he wouldn't put Eli in that situation, but he wouldn't put himself in it, either.

Rummaging in a cupboard for a box of mince pies his PA insisted he have — the rest of the contents from a huge hamper sent from a client had been divided up amongst the admin staff — Grey loaded up a tray and took everything through to the living room.

On his knees in front of the crackling fire, Eli was playing with Trevor who'd reverted back to the playful puppy he'd once been. Eli looked up and smiled, his eyes widening as a grin spread across his face.

"Mince pies. What a good idea. You can't have Christmas without mince pies. Or decorations for that matter." Eli glanced around the living room as he got up and sat on the squashy sofa next to Grey. "But at least you have a tree. If you can call it that." Eli wrinkled his nose, and looking over at the collection of twigs propped up in the corner, Grey had to agree.

Grey had blinked at the two delivery men who'd appeared at his door in the previous week. He had an annual order with the company who'd supplied it, the same one who supplied the office tree, and Grey had forgotten all about it. With its brutal minimalism, it hadn't been his choice, but his suggestion of something more traditional had been derided as little more than unimaginative and boringly suburban. It was cold and ugly, and as he glowered at it, Grey had no idea why he'd accepted the delivery and put it up; as soon as Christmas was over, it would be going to the recycling centre.

"I've got a food delivery coming tomorrow morning, which will contain more than a few concessions to the festive period." Grey hoped talk of Christmas treats would pull Eli's disdainful attention away from the tree. He was right.

Eli's face lit up in a huge grin. "Turkey? Christmas pudding? Brandy butter? And sprouts? Please tell me you've got sprouts?" Eli laughed as he took one of the little pies Grey offered him. "Ohhh, these are good. So buttery and sweet."

Grey's gaze dropped to Eli's lips, where a few golden crumbs clung before they were swept away by the tip of a pink tongue. Forcing his gaze away, Grey picked up his tea and took a gulp, wincing at the lava hot liquid. He cleared his throat.

"Not turkey, because I wasn't expecting company. And definitely no sprouts." He shuddered. "But yes to the rest of it. Stollen, too. I've even got a bottle of advocaat on order so I could make eggnog."

"*We* can make eggnog. I *lurve* eggnog. In fact I make the best snowballs on the planet. Hope you've got those syrupy little cherries, too?"

Grey laughed at the bright hope shining on Eli's face. Eli was almost bouncing with excitement. Deep in his chest, Grey's heart squeezed and clenched. Wasn't this how Christmas should be? Brimming with eagerness and anticipation? So different from last year's, when everything had come tumbling down around him.

"Yes, got those coming too," Grey answered, as he cleared his rough, dry throat.

"Excellent. This is turning out to be a real Christmas after all. So much better than what I had planned." Eli's joyous smile slipped from his lips as a frown wrinkled his brow. Grey fought to urge to smooth it away. "I was going to experiment with a pile of pizza and tuck into Benny's stash of artisanal vodka he thinks I don't know about."

Eli shrugged as his lips curved downwards, and Grey felt a surge of anger for the so-called friend and his arsehole boyfriend; Eli needed a distraction, and quickly.

"So tell me about your love affair with pizza. Pear, nuts, and honey aren't the usual suspects."

Eli concentrated on his tea, averting his gaze. Grey narrowed his eyes. Was Eli looking... shifty?

"It's my mission to try out as many topping combos as possible. Same for jacket potatoes. It's what I call market research."

Eli glanced across at him, settling for a moment before flitting away like a nervous butterfly. Intrigued, Grey couldn't help asking.

"Why?"

Eli returned his gaze to Grey, who had the uncomfortable, nervy feeling Eli was weighing him up, assessing whether or what to say in answer. Putting down his mug on the coffee table, Eli blew out a long breath, making his dark fringe flutter, and the doubt Grey had seen in his face melted away.

"I've got a plan I'm working towards, to have my own business. I'm getting there, but it's taking time, more time than I thought it would to be honest."

A worried frown scrunched Eli's forehead, and there it was again, that urge in Grey to smooth it away, to take care of whatever it was that was causing Eli to fret. He stilled his hand, as he stilled his tongue, and waited.

"I want to have my own catering business."

"You want to open a pizza restaurant?" It'd cost a small fortune to start up, and many businesses folded within a year. Doubt must have shown on his face, because Eli was staring at him, his mouth pressed into a thin line.

"No. Way too risky, and too much of a capital outlay, which I don't and won't have — not if I don't want to be saddled with debt. I'm talking about mobile catering. A mobile pizza and jacket potato business. I've got a business plan, and I've done my research so I know it can work."

There was defiance in his words, and in the steady, level gaze Eli locked onto Grey, as though challenging him to pour cold water on his idea. Grey would never do that, but he picked his words carefully.

"Then you've done a lot more than most people who start their own businesses. I'm all for self-employment, because after all I'm part of the club." Grey smiled, hoping to wipe away the defensive caste to Eli's face. It must have worked because Eli nodded, and when he spoke the slight defensive edge was gone.

"I know. Knowledge is power, right? That's why I'm trying out all these combos on my willing victims. To see if they work. You were won over, weren't you?"

Grey took a sip of his tea, which had grown tepid. It was his stalling tactic as much as it'd been Eli's. Yes, he'd been won over, completely and utterly, but not with pizza. Or maybe a little with the pizza.

"... festivals. So I know the sort of thing that sells."

Eli stared hard at him, his gaze intense. He was waiting for the answer to a question Grey hadn't heard.

"Festivals...?"

"Yeah. I spent most of my childhood and teens being taken to one festival or another. All over the country, going up and down in Mum and Dad's camper van. And you know what they all had in common?" Eli looked at him, as though willing the answer to spring from his tongue.

"I—"

"Food. Or, more accurately, not the right kind of food." Eli pulled his legs up and tucked his feet under him.

Excitement and a burning enthusiasm rolled off him as he warmed up to his theme. Grey was content to listen, content to enjoy this vibrant, animated version of Eli.

"Mongolian mountain goat curry is one thing, or tofu risotto, or whatever, but pizza and jacket spuds, *everybody* loves them." Eli began to count off the points on his fingers. "Easy and fast to cook if you've got the right set up. Inexpensive raw materials. Easy to eat. Endless meat-free and vegan toppings and fillings. At every festival or fair I went to, the queues for the pizzas and spuds were miles long.

"For a few months, I even worked for a friend of my parents' who had his own wagon. He made a mint. There are festivals and fairs going on all the time, all over the country, you can go from one to the other, and pizza and jacket potatoes work at any time of the year. It's what I want to do, to be in charge of my destiny."

Eli snorted out a laugh and glanced away as if embarrassed by his outburst of enthusiasm. Grey was filled with both adoration and admiration.

"I think it sounds like a good idea. Hard work—"

"I'm not afraid of working hard. Not for what I want. It's why I've been doing the Jolly Eventful stuff for the best part of a year. Or was. On top of the day job. All to save up for the equipment. My parents have said they'll help me, and they will if I ask, but they live what's not much more than a hand to mouth existence. I need to do this for myself."

"There's nothing wrong with asking for help, or accepting it when offered."

Grey's chest tightened. The words were meant for Eli, to let him know he didn't have to go it alone, that letting somebody take some of the weight wasn't a bad thing. Because some people wanted or needed to be another's rock, to hold them steady and take the strain. Grey coughed and cleared his throat.

"Day job? What do you do when you're not being an elf?" A very sweet and sexy little elf, Grey added but only to himself. Yet why hadn't he thought Eli had another job? Of course he would have, because seasonal gigs weren't going to pay the rent, or finance dreams and ambitions.

Eli groaned. "If you thought having to dress up as an elf, or a banana—"

"Banana?" Grey's brows arched.

"Yep. I've been the whole fruit salad at one time or another. Plus a hot dog, a chip, and even a microwave oven —no, don't ask." Eli glared at him, and Grey pressed his lips together. "In my day job, which, we were told last week would be undertaking some *streamlining* in the new year, I sell pet supplies. To pet shops. The Perky Pet Company, it's the biggest supplier of hamster consumables in the South East." Eli stared at him, his face impassive.

"Hamster consumables…?"

Eli's shoulders started to shake as be began to laugh. "Hamster wheels to you and me. But pet consumables of all kinds. Plus food, and non-vet supplied medicinals. I even have my own portfolio of customers. Each day, I have to ring around and enquire if they need any more worming tablets. Or maybe puppy wee mats. There was much excitement last month because we had a special offer on — flea powder, at half price. So, I reckon you can see why I might want to do something else with my life."

Grey laughed. "Yes, I think I can. You say you have a business plan—"

"I do. Fully thought out and costed."

"If you want an impartial view, I'd be happy to look over it at any time. You know where to find me."

Eli's eyes widened, as his mouth formed a small *O*. "Thank you. And you're right, I do know where to find you." He buried his face in his mug — surely any tea left was stone cold by now — but Grey didn't miss the flush that washed across Eli's cheeks.

Silence settled between them, but it didn't have time to take root as Trevor, fresh from a nap in front of the fire, decided he wanted to try and snuggle between them. His stubby legs made him clumsy, and Eli scooped him up but instead of settling in between, he climbed into Eli's lap and curled into a very comfortable looking ball.

"You've won him over. He's not very good with people, and he usually likes to keep himself to himself, but…" Grey bit off the rest; he might just as well have been talking about himself.

"Always had animals as a kid. It's why I ended up at The Perky Pet Company, where I'm carving out my stellar career." Eli snorted, as he poured all his attention onto Trevor. "You know, you should at least put up your Christmas cards."

"What?" Grey was taken aback by the sudden change in subject. Eli looked up at him as he stroked Trevor's short fur.

"They're on the side, by the tree. A big stack of them."

"The cards." Grey glanced over at the pile teetering on the edge of the bookshelf. He'd done nothing more than glance at them as he'd thrown each one aside. "I haven't had time to put them out."

Eli's arched brow was all the evidence Grey needed that his answer was lame and pathetic.

"It'd make the room look more Christmassy. So would some proper decorations on the tree — they'd at least cover it up."

"I get the distinct impression you don't like my tree." *Nor do I.* Grey kept a straight face.

"Only an impression? I mean, it's not exactly festive, is it? Even the three foot mini one I've got in my room at Benny's is better."

Grey looked across at the stark collection of branches in the corner. Minimalist and modern had been the supplier's description, hung with a few twisted pieces of metal that represented god alone knew what. It didn't look anything like the tree he knew growing up, all tatty and bedraggled as it was pulled from the attic on 1st of December of each year, and dressed with as much tinsel tat as it could support.

"I wanted something less—"

"Christmassy?" Eli laughed. "It looks like it should be in the foyer of a dental practice."

"Or the offices of a City bank?" He quirked his brows at Eli, before he took another look at the tree. It was truly horrible.

His gaze settled on the pile of cards; he supposed he should put them up.

"I'll help you, if you like?" Eli said, reading his thoughts, and before Grey could answer Eli deposited a disgruntled Trevor on the rug who, with a sharp yap, wandered from the room.

Eli picked up half the pile and began dotting them around. "Lots of robins this year." He held aloft a card depicting the red breasted bird perched on a snowy branch. "Do you think there are fashions in cards? One year, it's all Santas, the next reindeer. Or elves," he said laughing. "Oh, there's one here you haven't opened."

Eli handed over a large, embossed, cream envelope. Grey's heart fell, and a burning tingle raced up his arm as soon as his fingers touched it. He stared down at it, knowing exactly what it was, which wasn't Christmas cheer.

"Grey?"

"It's not a Christmas card." He tapped it against the fingers of his other hand. "I suppose," he said quietly, "I thought if it was out of sight and unopened, I could pretend it didn't exist." He felt Eli come and stand next to him, the younger man's closeness a comfort he didn't realise he needed.

"Then what—?"

"It's a wedding invite, for the summer."

"And you don't want to go? Can't you say you'll be away, or something?"

Grey stared down into Eli's upturned face. If only it were that easy.

"No, I can't."

"Why? If you really don't want to be there, don't be. Whose wedding is it, anyway?"

Grey didn't answer, as he tore open the envelope, his fingers acting before his brain could tell them to stop. He pulled out the card.

"*Mr. & Mrs. Carr request the pleasure of Grey Gillespie and guest at the wedding of their son David to Samantha...*" Grey golf balled his cheeks, his voice fading as he stared at the card.

"Who are David and Samantha, and why don't you want to go? One of them's not your ex, are they?"

Grey almost choked on his laugh. "No, but you're kind of in the right ball park. David's a friend of mine. A good friend."

Grey hesitated, the familiar hard knot of tension lodging in his stomach whenever he thought about—

He swallowed, as he met Eli's curious, concern filled eyes.

"David's brother... I was married to him. We've been divorced for just over six months."

CHAPTER ELEVEN

"Married?" Eli blinked up at Grey, unsure if he'd heard him right. Grey's next words were confirmation he had.

"Yes. David was my best friend at university and Peter was — is — his younger brother." Grey turned away and headed back to the sofa, his face tight, his fingers on the invite tighter. He sat down and looked at the invite. Eli sank down next to him.

"Why are you being invited? I mean, okay, you were friends with David, but if you and, and..."

"Peter."

"Yeah, sure. But if you and Peter have only been divorced for a few months, didn't your friend think it might be really, really awkward? For everybody?"

Grey's revelation had almost knocked Eli off his feet, and he'd staggered rather than walked across to the sofa, glad to collapse down onto it. Why had it affected him so much? It wasn't as if he knew much about Grey... But the stiffness in Grey's muscles, the hard scrunch of his brow screamed *tension* and made Eli want to sling his arms around Grey and whisper in his ear that he should tell this David character to shove his invite... Instead, he sat quietly and waited for Grey to speak.

"Do you want a beer?"

Grey jumped up, suddenly, making Eli lurch back. It wasn't what he was expecting to hear, but from the strained, tense expression on Grey's face, Eli knew they were both going to need a drink. He nodded, and Grey disappeared to the kitchen, leaving the now slightly crumpled invite on the arm of the sofa. Eli picked it up, holding it away from himself as though it might suddenly turn and bite him. Gingerly, he opened it up.

A village church, and afterwards at a golf club.

"Mr. Grey Gillespie and guest," Eli murmured.

Who would be Grey's guest? Whoever it was, he'd be a lucky guy. Grey looked good in a suit, tall and broad, blond and blue-eyed... Whoever he took with him, the guy should be proud to be on Grey's arm. If Grey decided to go, because Grey really shouldn't be accepting the invite, even if he didn't go so far as to tell his friend to stick it up his bum.

Grey returned with two open bottles of lager and handed one over. Taking the invite from Eli, he held it up.

"I can't not go. David and I go back too many years. He and I were good, close friends long before Peter and I got together. If I don't reply soon he'll be calling me every five minutes." He sat down and tossed the invite onto the coffee table, and turned the bottle around and around in his hands.

Eli huffed. "I'm sorry, but I don't see why you feel you have to. If he's such a good friend, he'd understand you saying no. He's probably expecting you to turn it down, because your—his brother—will be there, I assume?" Why was it so hard to for him to say *your ex-husband*? Eli gulped back on his lager, the icy cold alcohol stinging the back of this throat.

Why did you break up? What happened? Eli wanted to know why as much as he didn't.

"Of course he'll be there." Grey sighed, and to Eli it sounded like he had the weight of the world thrust suddenly upon his shoulders.

"When things got difficult between me and Peter, it was my side David took. The divorce didn't only damage me and Peter, it damaged the relationship between the two brothers, which was the last thing I wanted. They've managed to sort it out between them, and Peter's David's best man. But David's loyal, he doesn't forget who his friends are. I owe it to him to go. The wedding's not until the summer…"

Grey picked up the invite and stared down at it.

"We didn't have a bad break up, not that there's such a thing as a good one, so it's not as though there's a chance of some kind of scene erupting. Any dust that's still hanging about should have settled by then. It'll be awkward, but at least I'll have done the right thing by David."

Eli locked his hands together, to stop himself from grabbing Grey by the shoulders and giving him a hard shake.

Going to a wedding where his ex-husband would be swanning around, was not the *right thing*. But Grey wouldn't back out. Eli had come to know him enough to realise as much, because doing the right thing was important to Grey.

Eli sucked in his lower lip and clamped it between his teeth. It was why he was here, in the warmth and safety of Grey's home, because Grey had extended the right thing to him, even if the wrong done to him hadn't been Grey's to right.

"And guest?" Eli blurted out.

"I'm sorry?"

Eli nodded to the invite.

"It says *and guest*. You can't go on your own. In fact if you insist on going you should make a real splash. Be a bit… flamboyant."

Grey snorted. "I don't really do flamboyant."

"But if you do go—"

"There's no *if*. I'm going—"

"At least when you turn up, don't turn up on your own. Show Peter." Eli coughed. Why did the guy's name insist on getting stuck in his throat? "Show him you've moved on, that you've got somebody else in your life." *Me. I'd go with you. I could do enough* flamboyant *for the both of us.*

Grey stared at him, that same unreadable, blank eyed stare that was nonetheless sharp and piercing, and impossible to look away from. Eli swallowed… Oh shit, he'd said too much, he'd criticised the ex-husband if only obliquely when it really, really, absolutely really wasn't what he should be doing, because maybe Grey still loved him, so who was he to—

"Maybe you're right, about not going alone." Grey frowned, before he gulped back a mouthful of lager.

"You absolutely should take somebody. Somebody he doesn't know, so that you kind of make him wonder? The sweeter the arm candy, the more bitter the taste in his mouth."

Grey tilted his head as he looked at Eli, his eyes narrowing slightly. "I'm not interested in making him jealous, if that's what you mean. We didn't split up because there was somebody else — on either side. There were other issues." Grey's jaw tightened; he looked away and gazed into the fire.

Issues? What issues? Eli was aching to know, but he bit down on the questions he wanted to throw at Grey. It wasn't his business, he didn't know Grey well enough to ask about *issues*, and he didn't know Peter at all. Eli had never met the man, and likely never would, but he hated him anyway.

"Still reckon you should take somebody. There's nothing wrong with having a bit of moral support. And if it makes him at least a little bit curious, what's so bad about that?"

Grey's mouth opened, then closed, as though he thought better of what he'd been about to say.

"I don't know. Maybe."

Grey thrust his fingers through his hair, through the heavy hank Eli had seen him push out of his eyes so many times, and Eli had to clench his fists hard to stop himself from easing Grey's hand aside, to push back that thick, wavy hair himself.

"Well, it's what I'd do. And I'd make sure I shoved Mr. Candy in his face at every available opportunity. But then I'm not enough of an adult to *not* do something like that."

Grey smiled, but didn't reply, and they let the subject of weddings and ex-husbands drop.

"Let's see what's on the TV," Grey said, after a couple of minutes silence. With nothing but soap opera Christmas Specials, they decided to stream a film.

"Something feel-good and sappy, that wraps itself around you like a big fuzzy blanket. Pure escapism, because there's too much crap in real life." Eli settled back as Grey pulled up a list of films.

"*Elf*. Fancy seeing that?"

"Don't think so." Eli side eyed Grey, who was having a hard time from keeping the smile from his face.

They picked a film at random. Containing every cheesy Christmas theme and more, including cute kids and a lovely fluff ball of a puppy, it was the balm that soothed every part of Eli.

As its sugary warmth washed over him, Eli's eyes drifted closed, and he sighed as he relaxed into an enveloping warmth that was both tender and strong as it wrapped itself around him. Its pull was irresistible and undeniable, as the heavy weight that seemed to have sat on his shoulders and dragged him down for so long slipped away and disappeared. Eli snuggled deeper into sleep's protective arms, breathing in deep, breathing in the comforting aroma of warm spice and a dash of sharp winter orange. He sighed again, and slipped deeper and deeper into the all-enveloping darkness.

"Hey, time to wake up so you can go back to sleep."

A far off voice, warm, rich and enticing, like hot chocolate in front of a crackling fire, pulled Eli into a fuzzy wakefulness. He peeled his eyes open. Grey's face hovered above him, his lips lifted in a lopsided smile. Eli blinked to try to clear the fog from his sleep numbed brain. Why was Grey bent over him? He should have been sitting up, not—

"Oh." Eli struggled to pull himself upright, to lift his head from Grey's lap that he really didn't want to lift out of at all but his body, like his brain, had gone to sleep, and was even slower to wake up. Clumsy and uncoordinated, Eli tumbled to the floor.

"Oh, indeed. You fell asleep almost as soon as the film started, and flopped into my lap. At least now I can get my circulation going again."

Eli was pulled to his feet, staggering a little as the blood rushed to his head.

"You okay?" Concern flared in Grey's eyes and his voice, as his warm, strong hands held Eli still.

"I'm fine. Must have been more tired than I thought," Eli mumbled, his words disappearing in a yawn. "It's not been my usual twenty-four hours."

"For either of us," Grey said, so quietly it could have just been for himself. "Let me give you a hand upstairs. Don't want you falling."

Falling? But maybe it was already too late to stop him. The thought was evasive, slipping away before Eli's sleepy head could grasp it, as he let Grey steady him and support his weight as he led him out of the living room and upstairs.

CHAPTER TWELVE

As soon as Eli stumbled into bed, his brain played a cruel trick and woke up.

All he could think about was Grey's story. A wedding he refused to get out of, no matter how much he didn't want to go, and an ex-husband to face up to. Eli ground his teeth together at the thought of Grey toughing it out, all because attending was the *right thing* to do for his friend. It was crazy, but just another piece of evidence of how decent the man was.

Decent, kind, principled... Strong, decisive, in control... Good looking, hot, and sexy as fuck... Grey Gillespie was the perfect package, everything Eli yearned for in a man but never got.

Eli stared up at the ceiling, his head on his folded arms, mentally ticking off his exes. Most had been arseholes in one way or another. There had been a couple of guys who'd treated him with something approaching respect, leading Eli to believe they could be more, but when it came down to it none had wanted to stay around after the first few fucks that always left him feeling emotionally empty even when the physical itch had been well and truly scratched.

Eli swallowed down the sudden lump in his throat, as his fingers massaged the skin over where his heart lay... *Too needy, too clingy, too subservient.* Words, and others like it, that had been thrown at him in one way or another by the men who'd drifted through his life. He wasn't those things, because those words made him sound weak and weedy and he wasn't. How could he be all those things when he wasn't afraid to speak his mind and stand his ground, or at least most of the time? Eli sighed. He was, he supposed, a people pleaser, but that wasn't such a bad thing — was it?

He rubbed harder at the soreness he imagined in his heart, his fingers moving in ever decreasing circles. No, he wasn't weak because he fought life every step of the way even though there were times when it dragged the strength from him, leaving him to wonder if he had enough left to carry on the fight.

His fingers slowed, then stilled. What was so wrong in wanting a man of his own he could rely on, a man who'd gladly take some of his weight and support him when he needed another's strength? A man who'd hold him upright to stop him from falling when life pulled the rug from under his feet? A man who'd wrap his strong and protective arms around him, as he told him he had no need to worry, that he'd be taken care of?

"Grey wouldn't be like all those others," he whispered into the darkness.

Grey would treat the man in his life with thought and consideration, with care and respect. He'd protect and cherish. Hadn't he already done that, by taking him in, by making sure he had everything and more he needed? Eli could get used to a man like Grey... He could get used *to* Grey. The sudden, hard jolt in his chest sent a twitch down the entire length of this body.

No. No use thinking that way...

As soon as Benny was back, he'd be leaving and waving goodbye to Grey forever, as he worked out what he was going to do next. His time here was a blip in the flat line of his life.

Eli shifted again as his thoughts raced. He needed to thank Grey, to show his appreciation for all he had done for him, and was continuing to do. A smile tugged at his lips, but it fell away. There was one, very obvious, way but if he made an advance and Grey rejected him or even worse, thought Eli was trading himself as payment... Eli shivered, as ice settled in his gut, and froze his blood.

Yet, there had to be something he could do to show how much and how deeply he appreciated what Grey was doing for him, something that would make this Christmas good for Grey.

Christmas. There was very little sign of it in the house. A stark tree that looked like a bunch of twigs, and until he'd insisted they put them up, a pile of cards discarded on the side. Grey needed some brightness in his life, some warmth, even if only for a few days. Eli smiled as a plan began to take shape.

At last, his eyes closed as sleep stole over him. Christmas... There was time, time to make it a Christmas neither of them would ever forget.

CHAPTER THIRTEEN

Eli surveyed the garden as he held Trevor, hugging the small dog to his chest as though he were a furry hot water bottle. The kitchen was warm and filled with the savoury aroma of bacon and eggs, the yeasty smell of sourdough toast, and the underlying sweetness of almond croissants. Breakfast had been wonderful — the only problem was, he'd eaten it with only Trevor for company. The note Eli had found, propped up on the kitchen table over two hours earlier, had been apologetic: Grey was shut away in his home office, dealing with an unexpected work issue that couldn't be ignored or put off. His firm may have closed for Christmas, but Grey was very much open for business.

"I've got a plan, Trev," Eli whispered. "I'm going to bring a bit of the spirit of Christmas into this house, and Grey's going to help me."

Trevor looked up at him, his dark eyes as impenetrable and unreadable as Grey's could be. Eli smiled down at the dog, who answered with a good tempered bark. Eli turned his attention back to the garden. It'd stopped snowing, but the sky held a promise of more for later. It would give them time — but only if Grey wrapped up his work soon. It was already getting along for 11.30am, and daylight would be fading fast by mid-afternoon.

The door bell's sharp ring made Eli jump and Trevor barked and wriggled to be set down. The bell rang again a moment later as though whoever was on the other side of the door was quickly growing impatient. With no sign of Grey, Eli went to answer it.

"Mr. Gillespie?" the harried looking man on the step asked, a large collection of carrier bags by his legs.

"No, but—"

"Just taking a photo to show your order's been delivered. Run out of delivery boxes." The man gave a brief nod to the bags as he took the photo then turned on his heel and slipped and slid his way to the van. A second later he was gone.

"And a Merry Christmas to you, too."

In the kitchen, Eli unpacked the bags. Amidst the normal groceries there were plenty of concessions to Christmas. Mince pies, lots of them, and a pudding. Eli's heart dropped. A Christmas pudding for one. He put it aside and dug some more. Stollen, cream, and brandy butter. Chocolates. Eli smiled; Grey shared his own sweet tooth. Duck breasts — no turkey, not even for one, Eli remembered. Ready prepared pigs in blankets and sage and onion stuffing. Eli dug further, and chuckled. No Brussel sprouts. Advocaat and lemonade, and a jar of syrupy maraschino cherries. There were more than a few hints of Christmas, but Eli was going to make sure a whole lot more were added.

"Oh, good. It's arrived."

Eli jumped and swung around as Grey walked into the kitchen. Electricity tingled over Eli's skin. Grey, but not as Eli had seen him before. His hair was messy and mussed, as though he'd just tumbled out of bed, and dark gold stubble shadowed his jawline. A pair of jeans, soft-looking and well-worn, hugged his legs, their frayed ends resting on Grey's bare feet. An unbuttoned loose checked shirt was pulled on over a tight white T-shirt which stretched across Grey's broad and well defined chest, outlining his pecs and flat stomach. Eli stared, mesmerised, only knocked from his gawping when Grey pushed his fingers through the errant flop of his fringe.

"Are you okay?" Grey's brows puckered into a light frown, as he made a quick check through the items laid out over the counter.

"Er, yes. Fine."

Fine? Eli didn't feel anything like fine, not when Grey was standing so close to him, close enough for Eli to feel the warmth of Grey's body and to smell winter orange laced cologne.

Eli stumbled back a step. "It's stopped snowing," he croaked.

Grey looked up from putting the food away, and gazed out through the glass doors into the snow-bound garden. "Hmmm, more coming later though. This is just a breathing space."

A breathing space... That was definitely what Eli needed. He drew in a lungful of air, steadying himself. He had a plan, and he needed to get back to it.

"A breathing space is all we need."

"I'm sorry?" Grey turned from placing the last few things in the fridge. "I don't understand."

"Your house — your very lovely house, or at least your living room — is in need of a makeover. For Christmas."

"A makeover?" Grey cocked a brow.

"Yes. With just that odd tree you've got, it kind of looks like Christmas got chewed up and spat out. Christmas just isn't Christmas without decorations. I don't mean tinsel tat from World of Pound — although I like a bit, or a lot, of cheesy decorations — but I'm kind of guessing you don't."

"I wasn't really in the mood for decking the walls with boughs of holly this year."

"No, I guess not. But a few sprigs of greenery might be nice. Make it a bit more—"

"Christmassy and festive? I suppose... But the shops will be hell today, even if there is anything more to be had than the last sad pieces of tinsel."

Time to reveal my master plan...

"Wasn't thinking about the shops, but Hampstead Heath. We could go out and gather some holly and other greenery. Some pine cones, too. I used to do that with my granddad, and we'd drink hot chocolate and eat mince pies as we put it all up."

Eli's voice caught, as his granddad's mischievous, toothless smile filled his head. He still missed the old man, and always would.

"But only if you want to. Understand if you don't." Eli looked down, hoping Grey didn't see him blinking away the hot, salty tears.

"I think that sounds like the best idea I've heard in a long time."

Eli's head snapped up. It wasn't only the words, but the soft, caressing tone in Grey's voice.

"You do?"

Grey nodded slowly. "Yes. I didn't see any point in putting up decorations, not when it was just me here... I always liked to dress the living room. Peter was the one who favoured the minimalist approach." Grey shrugged. "But I think it sounds like a plan. Come on, before it starts to snow again."

CHAPTER FOURTEEN

The icy blast of wind was exactly what Grey needed. Work had become Grey's refuge in the last few months, so much easier than thinking about the train wreck of his life and how and what he might have to do to change it, but this morning he'd resented the time he'd had to spend locked inside his office, when there was somebody waiting for him he'd much rather be spending his time with.

Grey glanced across at Eli, trudging up the hill beside him, and suppressed a smile at the oversized coat enveloping him. Eli had point blank refused an overcoat when they had gone shopping, his rationale that although he needed the jeans and jumpers and boots, he wouldn't be sitting around in a warm house wearing a coat. Although he'd wanted to, Grey hadn't been able to argue against Eli's logic, and he'd been forced to concede, despite how much he'd wanted to spend his money to make things easier for his little elf.

His little elf... Tendrils of warmth coiled around Grey's heart, but he sucked in a long breath, forcing the freezing air deep into his lungs. He'd begun thinking of Eli more and more like that, more and more like his. But he needed to stop, as right and natural as it felt, because Eli wasn't his little elf, he wasn't his little anything, and to imagine otherwise was futile. Eli would be leaving in a matter of days, to pick up his life, as he would pick up his, leaving nothing more than a memory of when things were brighter and warmer than they'd been in a long time, when life felt good and purposeful once more. The warmth that had wrapped around Grey's heart turned a bitter, icy cold.

"I don't reckon this was one of my brighter ideas." Eli came to a stop, bending forward with his hands braced on his knees. "I thought I was fit, but this is like some kind of army assault course. Without the benefit of hot men in uniforms." He looked up, through his dark fringe peeking out from under the woolly hat he wore, his grimace morphing into a bright smile.

Adorable, so bloody adorable... Jesus, but he had to stop thinking like this.

"Look! Look, over there." Eli pointed, his excited words slicing through the thoughts Grey shouldn't be having. "Holly. There's loads of it, so we can fill up our bags." Eli tapped his pocket where a couple of the shopping carrier bags were stored away and gave a conspiratorial wink. "And we can get some ivy, too. Your living room is going to look like the centre fold spread of Stylish Christmas Homes. If that magazine doesn't exist, it should do. Come on." Laughing as he went, Eli slogged the last few steps to the top of the hill.

The bush was thick with holly, covered in fat red berries, and it wasn't long before they'd filled one of the bags to overflowing.

"Is it legal, what we're doing?" Eli asked, when they moved on to a clump of trees around which ivy twisted.

"Probably not. But if there's nobody here to report us…" Grey shrugged. He didn't know and he didn't care, because outside in the sharp air with Eli working beside him and looking way cuter than was good for Grey, was doing him more good than anything had done in a long time.

"In which case, let's see how much we can stuff in our bags."

A few minutes later they'd gathered together as much as they could carry home.

"I've never seen the Heath so empty. I thought there'd be lots of kids up here, building snowmen." Grey looked around him, at the Christmas card prettiness, squinting at the few people off in the distance. "But it's so cold, I —oooff!"

The thud hit him square between the shoulder blades. Grey spun around. Eli was standing a few feet away, his face bright with mischievous trepidation. One gloved hand was brushed with snow, the other, held aloft, clutched a snowball.

Grey narrowed his eyes, and Eli grinned.

"You really think you're going to get away with that? You were supposed to give me a warning. It's the cardinal rule of snowball fights."

Grey took a step forward, as Eli took one back, snowball still held high.

"No warnings, and take no prisoners. I fight dirty."

"Yeah? Well I fight bigger, faster, and stronger — and way dirtier."

Grey dropped the bags and swooped down, scooping

up a mound of wet snow. Eli's snowball whizzed past him, his aim less sure this time, before he turned tail and staggered through the thick snow, yelping and laughing as he tried to make his escape as Grey pelted his retreating back with expert overarm bowls.

Thank you, cricket practice…

Eli did his best to make as many snowballs as he could, but they fell short of Grey who continued launching his arsenal with military precision.

"Okay, okay, I give up." Eli, covered in an explosion of snow, held his arms up in surrender, all the time laughing.

"Stop? It doesn't work like that. I say when we stop, not you." Grey grinned as he stalked towards Eli. "You can't expect to throw a snowball at me and think you'll get away with it. Come on, Eli, time to take your punishment."

Grey leapt forward, but Eli anticipated him, and shot off down the hill, arms windmilling. Grey chucked the snowballs, one after the other in a ferocious volley but each fell shorter than the last as Eli ran fast.

Too fast.

Way too fast.

"Oh, shit." Grey bolted after him, slipping and sliding, but Eli, out of control, was putting distance between them. The downward slope of the hill was getting steeper, adding to Eli's uncontrollable momentum.

"Throw yourself down, to the side," Grey bellowed, but the wind whipped his words away. The slope began to level out, but not enough for Eli to regain control, and stop him from smashing into the huge tree in his path.

Grey surged forward, putting everything he had into catching up with Eli who was headed towards a head-on collision. Grey's long legs closed the gap, then a little more, just enough for him to throw all his weight behind a high leap, grabbing Eli tight, pushing him to the ground, the two of them tumbling in a tangled knot of limbs, snow sticking to their clothes, their hair, their faces. The tumbling slowed and stopped, under the tree's snow laden branches, just inches from its gnarled old trunk.

They lay panting, trembling, and dazed, arms wrapped around each other.

"My legs wouldn't slow down, I—I tried to stop but I couldn't."

Eli's voice was small and breathless. Grey untangled their limbs. Eli was hurt, he couldn't not be. He needed a doctor, The Royal Free Hospital was only minutes away...

"I'll call an ambulance." Grey fumbled for his phone, but Eli's hand, steadier than his voice, clasped his arm.

"I'm okay, and that's because of you. I'm a bit shaken up, got to admit, but the only thing really hurting is my pride."

"You need to be checked over."

Eli shook his head as, wincing, he pushed himself upright. He might have been white-faced and shaky but determination shone in his eyes.

"I've not broken or sprained anything, honest. The only thing I need is to get back and sit in front of the fire with a mug of hot chocolate, with maybe a mince pie or two. And some of those posh looking chocolates you had delivered earlier."

Eli smiled, but Grey knew it was held up on tight wires of willpower that could snap at any time.

"What you need is to be checked over by a doctor." Grey ground his teeth together, his jaw so tight the smallest increase in pressure would shatter it. Why wouldn't Eli concede and let Grey get him the care he needed?

"And spend hours and hours in A&E, only to be told to take some anti-inflammatories?"

Grey huffed, but Eli was probably right.

"The first thing you're going to do when we get home is have a hot bath with some essential oils. Then you can have the whole bloody box of chocolates."

"I'm feeling better already. Let's get the holly and stuff, and go." Eli nodded to the bags, abandoned further up the hill.

"Forget them. I need to get you home."

"And I need to see your living room decorated with more than a bunch of ugly twigs with bits of wire hanging from them. Go on, it's what we came here for. And honestly, I'm okay."

Grey didn't believe Eli was okay at all. Eli's face was bloodless, the tremble in his voice not disguised by his breezy claim that all was well. The near-calamitous accident, only just avoided, had shaken Eli to his core. If he wasn't going to agree to seeing a doctor, Grey would damn well make sure he was looked after at home. As fast as he could he retrieved the bags, reluctant to leave Eli alone a second longer than necessary.

"Come on, let me help you up."

"It's all right, I can—ohh!" Eli collapsed to the ground as his legs, too wobbly to hold him, buckled.

There was only one solution and Grey wasn't going to take no for an answer.

Pushing the bag handles into one of Eli's hands, Grey scooped him up in his arms.

"Grey, what—?"

"No arguments. I mean it."

"But…" Eli's protest faded to nothing as Grey tightened his arms around him.

Eli rested his head against his chest and closed his eyes as Grey held him tight and made his careful way towards home, hugging his precious cargo to him.

CHAPTER FIFTEEN

Eli snuggled down into the sofa, in front of the crackling fire, as Trevor dozed in his lap. His mind returned to what had happened out on the Heath. Not so much the accident, which had scared the living daylights out of him, and shaken him up more than he'd wanted to admit, but to what had happened after.

Grey, sweeping him up in his arms and holding him tight.

Eli swallowed, his mouth dry as he relived every single moment. He hadn't argued; there had been no point because Grey wouldn't have listened to him. But that hadn't been the only reason. He hadn't argued because he hadn't wanted to.

Wrapped in Grey's arms, Eli had never felt so safe and secure. So cherished. Eli closed his eyes and breathed in deep, just as he'd done when he'd burrowed in close to Grey's chest, hearing the hard, strong beat of Grey's heart. The sure and steady rhythm had calmed him, just as Grey's sure and steady arms around him had.

Wrapped up in Grey's soft dressing gown, after a soak in a hot bath, Eli lifted the collar of the dressing grown and gave it a sniff, drenching himself in the aroma of orange. But there was more, a base note of something deeper, warmer, and way more masculine and heady: the scent of Grey himself. Eli's heart twisted. Yes, the underscoring scent was all those things but it was so much more. It was the scent of care and consideration, of strength. It was a scent of a man who would keep him safe and warm, of a man who would pick him up when he fell.

And don't I feel like I've been falling, far too deep and for far too long?

On his lap, Trevor shifted and snuggled closer, and Eli slowly ran a hand over the little dog. Life, beyond the safety of Grey's four walls, was little more than a hard, never ending grind. He was a hamster on a wheel, always moving but never getting anywhere.

"Do you think I'm a fraud, Trev? Because when I feel brave enough to take a really close look at myself, that's what I think."

Trevor snored softly.

Eli stared at the fire. Fraud. That was what he was, to himself more than anybody. He hid behind a breezy approach to life, his confidence nothing more than a façade that threatened to crumble and fall if prodded and poked too hard. His home wouldn't be his home for much longer and his job might not be there in the New Year. What money he'd scrimped and saved would have to be spent on surviving before going towards realising his ambitions to be his own boss.

A potato and pizza wagon. It sounded so… small. Benny and Lenny had laughed, deriding his idea when he'd told them, but they hadn't been the only ones and it was why he kept it to himself. Until he'd told Grey. Grey, who hadn't laughed or looked at him as though he'd lost his mind. It wasn't much of an ambition, not in the grand scheme of things, but it was his, yet that sharp, clear vision he'd always tried to focus on now seemed blurred and a lot further away.

Eli closed his eyes against the sudden upwell of tears. Today, everything had been different. Winded and shaken, all the worry, all the tension, all the hollow feeling in the deepest, darkest place in his heart that made him feel so, so lonely, it'd all been swept away as Grey had cradled him in his arms and held him close.

The living room door creaked and Eli snapped his eyes open as Grey shouldered the door wider, carrying a large tray.

"How do you feel now? Better for your bath?" Grey smiled as he set the tray on the coffee table, laden with steaming mugs of hot chocolate and a selection of sweet Christmas treats.

"Much better, thanks. I've got a few bruises, but that's all to show for my spectacular display. I was like that cheese they roll down the hill in Gloucestershire, but the human variety."

Eli forced a laugh. Easy, breezy, just as ever. But Grey didn't laugh, as he sat next to Eli and looked at him with his deep, assessing, disorientating stare which felt like it was reaching all the way down into Eli's soul.

"If you'd have hit that tree you'd have been seriously injured. Or worse."

Eli looked down, unable to hold Grey's intense gaze.

"Yes. I was lucky you were there to save me."

"Somebody had to."

Trevor twitched, barked himself awake, slipped from Eli's lap and made his tail-wagging way out of the living room. In the grate, the flames hissed and crackled as a log shifted, sending up a spray of sparks. From outside, the muted sound of a car door slamming, followed by laughter.

Eli plastered a smile onto his face, so damn bright and breezy, as he looked up and forced himself to meet Grey's gaze.

"Thank you, for scraping me off the ground. I may not be very tall, but I'm no light weight. Couldn't have been easy lugging me down the hill like some giant sack of spuds." Eli smiled wider, in the hope Grey would laugh, but instead Grey kept his level, serious gaze fixed on him.

Grey shook his head. "You were no weight at all, and like I said, somebody had to rescue you."

Rescue you... The words wound their way around Eli, warm and caressing, like the softest blanket. Eli swallowed as the air in the room grew denser and heavier, as his pulse picked up and his skin goose bumped.

Rescue... me.

The world had contracted to this one room, where only he and Grey existed. Slowly, they leaned into each other as though pulled by an invisible thread. Heads tilted, lips parted, Eli's eyes fluttered to a close, ready, needing, craving the kiss and whatever else it might bring.

Warm, strong hands rested on his cheeks, holding him still. Eli's eyes flew open.

"What?"

Grey shook his head.

"It wouldn't be right."

"B—but…" Eli stammered as confusion fogged his brain.

Grey, still holding his face between his palms, stroked his thumbs across his cheekbones, wrenching a sigh from deep inside of Eli.

"I don't understand." But as Grey's gaze roamed across his face, taking in every inch of him, in his heart Eli did understand.

Grey gave a gentle huff, as his thumbs continued their soft sweep across Eli's cheekbones.

"You're here with me because you were in need of help. Dire need. Need which was caused—"

"No, you're not to—"

Grey pressed a finger to Eli's lips, and it was everything Eli could do not to suck that finger deep into his mouth.

"All the time you're here, you're under my care and protection. What sort of man would I be if I tried to take advantage of the situation? That's not care and protection, it's an abuse of power. There's a difference, and I won't cross the line."

"But—"

"No, Eli. It's how I am. It's who I am." Grey sat back, taking all this warmth with him.

Eli's hands itched to pull him back, telling him to screw the line because lines were meant to be crossed, but the resolute set to Grey's face had Eli balling them into tight fists.

Decent, when all he wanted was to get *indecent*… But wasn't it Grey's decency that made him the man he was?

Eli sagged deeper into the sofa cushions, as deflated as a week-old balloon. His gaze fell on the bags of greenery, leaning next to the ugly Christmas tree. The greenery, the whole reason they'd gone out in the first place.

"Decorations." Eli nodded to the bags.

"What? No. Not now, not after what you've been through." Grey frowned and shook his head.

Which was nothing to what I'm going through now…

"I'm fine. Honestly." *Such a liar…* "I'll be back in a minute."

Eli jumped up, biting down on his lower lip to stop himself from wincing, and rushed from the room before Grey could protest, thoughts of decency, care and protection chasing after him.

CHAPTER SIXTEEN

With a heavy heart, Grey watched Eli flee from the living room. He was tempted to run after him and drag him back, pull him into his arms and carry through on the kiss he'd only just about had enough will power to resist.

Grey scrubbed his hands down his face. Resist. He didn't want to resist, Eli didn't want to resist, so what was the problem? But he knew what it was. If they'd kissed, if they'd succumbed to so much more — and there was no doubt in Grey's mind they would have — he would always have the lingering doubt that Eli, deep down, had given himself out of a sense of gratitude and obligation. And Grey could never, ever allow that to happen.

He pinched the bridge of his nose. What was it Peter had said, one of his final shots sent deep into Grey's heart? Grey wanted to control and take charge, he wanted to smother. And maybe that's what he did want to do, if taking control and being in charge, and smothering, meant caring and making sure the man in his life was cared for and kept safe. He'd known Eli for no time at all, but already Grey was stepping on that same path, the one Peter had turned away from.

The door opened and Eli slipped inside, and as Grey looked up at him, all he could do was wonder why he'd pulled back.

Eli had got dressed in the clothes they'd chosen together. In dark jeans, and a loose moss green shirt, how Eli could pull off looking relaxed and comfortable Grey had no idea when he was feeling anything but, yet, the slight flush that clung to Eli's cheeks, through which the shadow of that delicious dark scruff showed, was the only indication of what had happened just minutes before.

Eli picked up one of the bags and stared at it, before he sighed and looked up, his gaze direct as his lips lifted in a small, wry smile.

"You're probably right about, well, you know."

"I am." *Am I?*

The fire hissed and spat in the hearth, and Grey's heart hammered out a hard, fast beat.

Probably…

"Yeah. Reckon so. Awkward, you know?" Eli shifted from foot to foot, as he clutched the bag.

"Eli—"

"Let's get on with it." Eli pasted a big smile across his face which Grey didn't believe in at all. "If we're going to give this room a bit of the old festives we should get started." Eli emptied the bag of its greenery into a pile on the floor, the action a huge sign that read *I don't want to talk about this anymore.*

Grey nodded, not knowing what to say — not that Eli

seemed to want him to say anything — as he grabbed the other bag and emptied it next to the pile Eli was sorting through.

They worked in silence for a couple of minutes that felt like hours, bursting with all the awkwardness they were meant to be backing away from.

"You know what we need?" Eli said, breaking the silence.

Grey didn't trust himself to answer.

"Some carols."

"What?" Grey looked up. Eli's gaze was calm and steady but his front teeth, clamped down on his lower lip, showed it up for the illusion it was.

"Carols. Christmas without carols is like sausage without mash. You find a station playing carols and I'll make a start."

The sounds of Christmas smoothed over the cracks. Grey let the traditional carols wash over him, as they set about decorating the room under Eli's supervision, the task soothing and calming. Garlands of red berried holly tumbled down from the fireplace mantel whilst bunches were bound together, using the ivy as string, and placed on the hearth, along with a glass bowl filled with pine cones.

Grey stepped back and looked at their handiwork. Already the room felt cosy and festive and more like a home once more.

"It looks lovely. I didn't realise just a few bits of holly—"

"Would make such a difference? Now it really does feel like Christmas."

Eli smiled as he stepped in beside Grey. The light

outside was fading fast and Grey had turned the lamps on, their soft light bathing the room in a warm and golden glow. Grey cast a glance at Eli, his breath catching as the buttery light shone on his hair, picking out the strands of dark copper and making them glow bright like the smouldering logs in the grate.

"Not sure we can do much to improve that ugly tree of yours, though."

"It's not ugly. It's contemporary minimalism."

"Which translates as ugly." Eli frowned in thought. "We've got a few bits left, but do you have any bright coloured scarves? We could wrap some around it, to disguise its profound and utter nastiness." Eli stared at him with a deadpan expression.

"Do I look like a man who owns a limitless supply of colourful scarves?" Grey raised a brow in challenge.

Eli chuckled, the low, throaty sound sending a delicious shiver down Grey's spine.

"Who knows? You could have hidden depths."

Grey doubted it. He didn't have scarves, but—

"I've got a reel of red ribbon. I think it might be in my office." Red ribbon bought to wrap a special gift, last Christmas. He should have thrown it out, but as Eli's eyes sparkled with delight Grey was very glad he hadn't.

A couple of minutes later, and with a gleeful smile, Eli wrapped the scarlet velvet ribbon around the tree, transforming it into something worthy of the season. Grey smiled as he watched Eli throw himself into the task he'd set. The awkwardness of earlier had at last melted away, replaced by Eli's almost childlike joy.

"There, that looks better, but it needs something on the

top." Eli looked up at the tree. "And I know what." With deft fingers, he tied a large and elaborate bow with what was left of the ribbon, and held it out with a triumphant grin. "And before you ask, I once had a holiday job in a fancy gift shop, and they taught me how to make bows and stuff for gift wrapping. Let me stand on a chair and I'll fasten it to the top."

Before Grey could stop him, Eli dashed from the room, returning moments later with a kitchen chair.

"No, not after that fall you—" Grey swore. Eli was already on the chair. "You shouldn't be doing this, not after your tumble earlier." Grey frowned as Eli attempted to attach the bow.

"Told you, the thing that hurt most was my pride."

Grey's frown deepened and he pressed his lips together. He'd seen how shaken Eli had been, had felt him tremble in his arms. His hands burned to lift Eli off the chair and set him on the sofa but instead he drew in a deep breath and let it go slowly as he stood close, ready to catch Eli if he threatened to fall.

Eli reached for the tree's pinnacle, the movement pulling his shirt free from the waistband of his jeans. Just a couple of inches, it was enough to show dark bruising and Grey bit down on his tongue, sending a spasm of pain through him.

Not quite able to reach, Eli pushed himself onto his toes and wobbled.

"I just need to reach a little higher…"

Grey grabbed him hard, clamping his hands to Eli's hips.

"For god's sake, come down from there. Isn't one fall in a day enough for you? You're covered in bruises." Grey pushed the words out through gritted teeth, each one as hard as iron.

Eli stilled and looked down at him, their eyes locking.

"Not covered. Just a few. Honest. Maybe the snow cushioned the worst of the fall?" Eli looked away, taking just a couple of seconds to fix the bow in place. "Done—"

Grey pressed his lips into a harder, tighter line. Yes, Eli was done — done with risking taking another tumble. Sliding his hands to Eli's waist, he lifted him from the chair and planted him safely on the floor.

"Oh!" Eli's eyes widened before he blinked. "A bit battered and bruised or not, I could have got down on my own."

"More than a bit. Your shirt, it's come loose." Before he could think, before he could begin to stop himself, Grey trailed the backs of his fingers over Eli's exposed skin. Eli's gasp was a burst of searing electricity, and Grey stumbled back as though burned. "I'm sorry, I shouldn't have—"

"No, it's okay. Er, yeah, I've got a few bruises…" Eli dipped his head as he made a mess of shoving his shirt back in.

Trevor padded into the room, yapping to announce his presence. Eli bundled the dog into his arms, and buried his face in his fur, looking up at Grey through his long dark lashes.

"I, erm, think we deserve a treat after all our hard work, don't you?"

"A treat?" Grey had no idea what Eli was talking about, because all he could feel was the tingling heat in his hands from that illicit touch.

"Hmm, some eggnog and more mince pies. And maybe stollen. Followed by some more chocolates."

Grey barked out a laugh. Sugar laden treats, none anywhere near as sweet and delicious as Eli, but way, way safer.

CHAPTER SEVENTEEN

An early dinner replaced Eli's suggested sugar fest. Grey had cooked the meal, batting away Eli's offer of help as he ordered him to rest. A simple chicken stew served up with buttery mashed potatoes. Maybe not the festive treats Eli had been hankering for, but the satisfied look on Eli's face when he finished his last mouthful made Grey's heart glad. The two of them together, in the warm kitchen, was perfect domesticity.

"That was lovely, thank you. I thought you said you weren't much of a cook?" Eli stretched and yawned with feline grace.

Grey shrugged. "The few things I do, I do well."

It wasn't a boast or a brag, but the simple truth. Peter had been the cook out of the two of them.

Peter… Just days before the smallest thought of his ex would have pulled him down like a brick in water, but in the warmth of the kitchen, with Eli, the man who'd been his world for so many years felt far away, out of focus and indistinct

"Well, I'm sure there are lots and lots of things you do well." Eli's lips lifted in a dark smile, but his eyes held a glint of mischief.

"Eli," Grey growled.

Eli laughed. "I know, I know. I'm being a bad boy."

A bad boy… A pulse of heat shot through Grey and his cock stiffened, tightening the front of his jeans. He was more than sure Eli was capable of being a bad boy. A very bad boy. Grey shifted in his seat, trying and failing to push away images of Eli being bad for him.

"Grey? You're miles away. What are you thinking about?"

Eli was standing over him, holding their plates as he smiled down at Grey. His spellbinding eyes appeared darker than normal. Darker, and watchful, as though watching all of those thoughts Grey couldn't get out of his head. Thoughts he was determined they were *not* going to act upon, yet, as he met Eli's gaze, Grey's determination no longer felt quite so resolute.

"I can make some coffee, if you like, and then we can have all the Christmas food you wouldn't let me have earlier, for pudding." Eli laughed, the sound bright and clear, sweeping away the dark heat of moments before.

Maybe he'd imagined whatever it was he thought he'd seen… Maybe.

"Or, I've got some brandy if you'd rather?" Grey blurted out.

Eli nodded with enthusiasm. "Just for medicinal purposes, of course. After my near death experience from earlier."

They took a plate, piled high with Christmas sweet-ness, into the living room. The fire danced in the grate, the flames licking the logs like long red tongues. Grey pulled out a bottle and a couple of glasses, and poured the deep golden spirit.

"Hmmm, perfect." Eli closed his eyes as he sipped, the tip of his tongue sweeping across his lips, lapping up the drink and leaving a damp sheen on his plump red lips.

Grey swallowed, unable to look away. Full, red lips aching to be kissed. He could kiss them, he yearned to kiss them, kiss them and more. His grip on his glass tightened and he bit hard against the inside of his cheek, so much that he winced and tasted the metallic tang of blood.

No. He had offered Eli a home for Christmas, and there was no way he was going to insist on rent Eli might feel obligated to pay.

Grey gulped at his brandy. The alcohol stung the bite on the inside of his cheek, and burnt his throat, making his eyes water.

"I never used to like spirits, or not until I found Benny's secret stash."

Grey jumped at Eli's sudden words. Curled up on the sofa, Eli smiled, his startling two-tone gaze resting on Grey.

"I think it might be one of the reasons he wants me gone." Eli's face fell, and his shoulders slumped, before he forced the smile back on to his lips which didn't reach his eyes. "But that's for the New Year, not now, because now is the time for that last mince pie, which is looking very lonely on its own."

Eli groaned as he took a bite, his eyes fluttering to a close. Golden crumbs clung to his lips and he lapped them away. But he missed a piece, and it took everything Grey had to not lean forward and kiss the evidence away.

Grey's pulse thumped hard and fast. He was hot, and his skin tingled as his cock filled to bursting, and pressed hard against the zip on his jeans. It would be so, so easy to throw aside all the self restraint it was becoming more and more difficult to fight against. His breath stuttered in his chest. Eli wanted him as much as he wanted Eli, their mutual desire making the air around them thick and heavy, so what was the—?

Grey's mobile rang, a hard and heavy axe blade slicing through his fevered thoughts. Eli's eyes shot open. The grey and the green of his irises were foggy and dazed as if he'd just emerged from a deep sleep.

"Aren't you going to get that?"

Grey swore as he fumbled his phone from his pocket, and jabbed accept without looking at the caller ID.

A voice he'd know anywhere said his name.

Grey's gaze landed on Eli. Grabbing the empty plate, Eli jumped up from the sofa and disappeared from the living room.

"Grey? Grey are… there?" Peter's voice, on the other end of the line, broke up. "Sorry… bad line. Must be… weather. I want… about… mas."

"I can't hear you." *And I don't want to, Peter, not now.*

"Christmas… I don't… your own."

Grey pulled the phone from his ear and stared at it. He'd filled in the missing words. Christ, Peter wasn't asking him to spend Christmas with him — was he? He needed to kill that idea right now.

"Christmas is sorted. I've got a friend with me," he shouted, over the breaking connection.

"Friend? Who? Have… somebody?"

The connection was poor, but not poor enough to disguise the startled curiosity in Peter's voice.

"Nobody you know. Happy Christmas, Peter—"

"Grey? I can't hear. Who—?" The line died before Grey could kill it.

Powering his phone down, Grey turned it over and over in his hands. It had been a surprise to hear Peter's voice again, or as much of it as he could, but not the stomach churning, heart racing, pulse thumping shock it would have been only weeks, or even days, before. He strode to the living room door and slung it open.

"You can come back now," he called, as he waited on the threshold.

Down the long passageway which led to the kitchen, Eli poked his head around the door, before he emerged, holding a replenished plate.

"Stollen." Eli held the plate up as he came to a halt in front of Grey. "Dessert is a series of courses. We'll finish with chocolates."

Grey grinned and shook his head. "Is there no end to your sugar addiction?"

Eli tilted his head as though in deep and serious thought, but a tiny smile danced across his lips.

"No."

They took up their places on the sofa again, and Grey waited for the question he knew would come.

"Was that—?"

"Peter. Yes. The line was terrible but I got the distinct impression he was going to ask me to spend Christmas with him. He thought I was on my own, so I suppose it was a pity call."

"Ohhh… So, did you tell him you rescued an elf?"

Grey laughed and shook his head. "No. I told him I had a friend staying, nobody he knew, but he'll be wondering. I wouldn't be surprised if he came up with some excuse to try and call round. It's as well I changed the locks."

"Do you really think he'd try and let himself in?" Eli's eyes widened in shock and horror.

"Hmm, possibly."

Eli sucked in his lower lip and Grey waited, already knowing what Eli was working up to say.

"Would you like him to come round? I mean, do you miss him?"

Grey's reply fell from his lips before he could give himself time to think. "If I'd been asked that just a week ago, I'd have said yes. Or I think I would. But there's no way back for us. In the end, he didn't want what I had to give. But all that's in the past."

In the past. The words thumped into Grey's chest. It was exactly where Peter was, and where he was going to stay. It wasn't the first time he'd said those words but it was the first time he'd meant them.

The impulse, sudden and overwhelming, pressed down on Grey. Jumping up and wrenching open a cupboard door beneath the bookshelves, he pulled out the framed photo which had once taken pride of place in the living room.

"Meet Peter Carr, the former Mr. Peter Gillespie."

CHAPTER EIGHTEEN

Eli stared down at the photograph of Grey and Peter, faces pressed together as they grinned for the camera. It was a beautiful photo, black and white with an arty vibe. The grooms were handsome, they looked ecstatically happy and in love, and Eli's stomach knotted in a jealousy he had no right to feel.

"He's stunning." It felt like such an understatement. Like Grey, Peter could have graced the cover of any men's style magazine.

"He did some modelling in his teens and early twenties. He started to get noticed, but he stepped back. It wasn't the life he wanted, he said."

A model, with the world at his feet and who gave it up for—What? For love? For Grey? As Eli stared at the beautiful man whose face shone with joy on his wedding day, why it had all gone wrong clawed at him.

"Why did you split up?" The words that were not his to ask, however much he wanted to know the answer, burst from Eli. "I'm sorry." Eli's cheeks throbbed with embarrassment. "It's not my business, I shouldn't—"

"It's okay. It boils down to what I said a couple of minutes back."

Eli scrunched his brows together as he tried to remember, and then it came back to him.... *He didn't want what I had to give.*

Grey took the framed photo back and placed it on the coffee table. He leaned forward and rested his arms on his knees, leaving a few seconds before he turned his head to look Eli square in the face.

"In the end, modelling wasn't the only life he didn't want." Grey snorted. "I, however, wanted to give him everything I believed he did want. Not only materially, which I could easily do because putting it bluntly I was the one with the money. It was more than that, way more."

"More? What do you mean?"

Deep inside Eli, the answer stirred. Because he knew, in every fibre of his being, and it warmed a secret part of him, a secret, shadowy, craving part of himself.

Grey turned his head away and stared into the fire, now smouldering red embers. Silence filled the room. There was no awkwardness, no embarrassment, only a kind of hush as Eli waited for the answer he knew would come.

"I wanted to care for him and keep him safe. Every second of the day. I wanted to protect him." Grey huffed a laugh, and shook his head. "What it was I wanted to keep him safe from, I don't know. All I know is that I did. It's who and what I am, it's not something I can switch on and off. He knew that, and he accepted all I offered him. From the very start. I really believed it was what he wanted, too. Until the day came when he didn't."

128

The muscles in Grey's face tightened as his brows pulled together.

"He said he felt smothered by me. And powerless. That knocked me sideways. What Peter wanted and needed — or what I thought he did — I was committed to giving him. Willingly. His happiness was my priority."

Grey exhaled a long breath, and Eli's heart squeezed with all the sadness it carried.

"What it all came down to, in the end, was that he'd fallen out of love with me."

A lump lodged deep in Eli's throat. His mouth was dry and his heart thundered in his chest, crashing into his ribs. Care and protection, to be the undisputed centre of another's world, it was the deep, warm bath Eli had dreamed so many times of sinking into where all the aches and pains of life would be soaked away. It was what he'd so often longed for, when all life seemed to give him were freezing cold showers.

"Then the man's a fool. He didn't deserve you, still doesn't, and you're better off without him."

Grey turned his head, his eyes shadowed, the set of his jaw stiff as he pushed his lips together in a thin line.

The only thing Eli could hear in the warm, still room was the hard thud of his heart and the rush of blood whistling through his veins. He'd said too much, and it was too late to grab the words back, but he didn't want to, because the former Mr. Gillespie, the man who'd been honoured to take Grey's name, didn't deserve as much as a hair from Grey's head.

Grey's face softened and he shifted, revealing the soft light shining in his eyes.

"I've been trying to tell myself that for the last six

months, but here and now is the first time I've really believed it." Grey picked up the photograph, and ripped it from its frame.

"What—?"

"Something I should have done months ago."

Eli gasped as Grey balled the photo up and threw it on the fire, where flames hissed and spat, and turned it into no more than a pile of ash.

"Wow, that was…"

"I needed to do it, I can see that now."

Grey gazed down at him. In the softly lit room and with the fire, now fed and burning bright, casting a flickering glow across him, Grey looked wild, free and strong. His eyes bored into Eli's, magnets drawing him to Grey, and Eli was powerless to resist their pull.

Eli stood. Stepping up to Grey, he met his irresistible gaze.

"What else do you need to do?"

Eli placed his hands on Grey's chest. The beat of Grey's heart, and the warmth of his skin through the shirt was an invisible cord binding them together.

In the warm, shadowy room it was just them, their troubles past and present locked outside in the cold where they belonged. Here and now there existed only Grey and him, one man who only wanted to hold and protect, the other wanting only to be held and cared for.

"This."

Eli sighed as Grey cupped his face with his warm, steady hands. Grey's gaze travelled over his face. Eli shivered. It was as though Grey were drinking in every part of him. Grey's gaze settled on Eli's lips and as he tilted his head, Eli mirrored him, closing his eyes as he gave himself up to the kiss he wanted more than life itself.

Their mouths melded together as Eli melted into Grey's tall, strong body, his heart all but bursting into flame at the first electric, searing touch of tongues.

Grey slid his arms around Eli's waist, pulling him in tight as he deepened the kiss. Wet, sloppy, their breaths coming in fast shallow gasps. Want, need, desire, lust, they were all there in the kiss that grew hotter and deeper with every beat of their hearts. Grey's hands slipped to Eli's backside and Eli gasped as he was tugged hard against Grey, their swollen cocks bumping and grinding as they rocked into each other in heated desperation.

A trembling groan, which in some still rational part of his brain Eli knew had been dragged from him, broke the kiss. Panting hard, their mouths wet and slack, Eli and Grey stared at each other. Grey, with a deep flush colouring his cheekbones, his lips bruised and swollen and his eyes dark and craving, he was wild and wanton, strong and masculine, and everything Eli not only wanted, but needed, in the deepest and most hidden part of himself. He hooked his fingers around the buckle of Grey's belt, ready for everything that was to come next.

Their lips crashed together as fingers fumbled for buckles, belts, and buttons, all the time their mouths joined in a breathless, desperate kiss.

"What the fuck," Grey growled as he broke loose, ripping aside Eli's shirt, sending buttons pinging in all directions.

"Hey, I liked that shirt." Eli laughed, but he was stopped by another deep, soaking kiss that sucked the words from his mouth. He liked the shirt, but he liked this way better.

Grey's hands were everywhere. Hard, hot, commanding, pushing Eli's jeans and underwear down to his ankles. Eli stumbled out of them, and kicked them aside. His eager, aching cock bounced against his belly, leaving a thin thread of pre-cum trailing from the slit on the engorged, bulbous head. His hand wound around his shaft as Grey discarded what was left of his own clothing.

Eli's breath caught in his throat and his hand stilled.

Jesus...

Grey stood before him, his body gloriously naked.

Muscled but not muscle-bound, the V of his lower abs clear and defined and leading down to a cock that reared up, flushed and pulsing, from a thatch of dark blond pubic hair. Eli's mouth watered and his stomach clenched hard as his already erratic heartbeat cranked up, knowing that here and now, whatever Grey's history, this man was *his* and his alone.

Eli was bumped out of his reverie as Grey wrapped his hand around his wrist and eased him down onto the soft and silky rug in front of the fire.

"And here was me, thinking you were going to sweep me up in your arms and carry me up to bed." Eli laughed, but he could feel and hear the tremor in his voice.

Grey's eyes narrowed as he gently pushed Eli down on his back and straddled him.

"Are you a closet romantic, Eli? Hmm? Because I am. What could be more romantic than making love in front of a log fire?"

Making love... The words wound around Eli's heart and hugged it close.

He'd never made love, only fucked and screwed, the thrill fun but fleeting. An ice-cold drink on a hot day, it slaked the thirst, forgotten as soon as it was finished with, until the thirst returned and it started all over again.

Eli shivered as Grey's warm breath danced across his lips.

"I... *oohhh*," he sighed as Grey brought his lips to his neck and peppered him with tiny, tickling kisses.

Eli dissolved into a pile of goo. Nobody ever kissed him there, on the nervy, sensitive skin on the side of his neck. Nobody had ever bothered to take the time to melt him like this, nobody except Grey, who just seemed to know...

"Oh, g—god..." Eli's breath stuttered in his chest as Grey kissed his meandering way down his body. The base of his throat, and over his chest, where Grey came to a stop and rimmed one nipple, then the other, with the tip of his tongue, his deep chuckle sending a delicious shiver through Eli's body.

Eli could come like this, just this, just from Grey's teasing kisses that found all those spots that made him squirm and gasp and tremble with need. His cock ached, the skin stretched hot and tight, and Eli's hand fumbled for himself.

"No."

Eli's eyes snapped open, his hand freezing, obeying the hard denial in Grey's voice.

Grey's lips lifted in a dark smile as he locked his hand around Eli's wrist, pushed his arm above his head and pinned it to the floor. Grey stared down at him as he hovered above Eli, his heavy hair falling forward.

With his free hand, Eli reached up and ran his fingers

through it, his heart stuttering when Grey's smile softened. His eyes, though dark with want and desire, shone with something softer and gentler.

"I don't want to rush this, Eli. We've got all the time in the world, and I want us to take it."

Grey resumed his slow journey down Eli's body. Across his stomach, which quivered with every feather light touch Grey let fall on his heated skin, as he snaked his way towards Eli's straining cock. Eli's hips lifted, his cock bumping against his stomach as it sat up and begged for Grey's mouth.

Yes, yes, yes... Grey was drawing closer, his hot breath already caressing his pulsing cock head, those full red lips ready to wrap themselves around Eli's desperate—

Eli whined as Grey's kisses swerved away and headed towards the crease at the top of his thigh.

"W—what?" Eli's voice shook with desperation and confusion as he levered himself up onto his elbows and stared down at Grey.

Grey looked up, his lips curving up into a wicked grin.

"You fucker," Eli said, but there was no venom in his voice, and no strength either as Grey, still smiling, dropped his head and nuzzled and kissed.

Eli forgot why he'd been peeved, as he collapsed back on the rug and gave himself up to every one of Grey's kisses and nuzzles, tiny licks and tinier nips, sighing and moaning, every part of his body thrumming with pleasure.

Grey made the return journey along the other side of Eli's body, his lips brushing Eli's in the lightest of kisses. Eli chased the kiss, needing the connection once more of their mouths. Grey pulled back, just out of reach. Eli swallowed a screech of frustration as he glared at Grey. This wasn't fair. This wasn't fair *at all*.

"You're torturing me, you git."

"Torturing you?" Grey raised a brow, his gaze dark as his lips twitched a smug smile. "You don't sound or look like you're being tortured."

Grey, still straddling him, rocked forward and his cock, as hard and leaking as Eli's own, dragged over his, making Eli hiss at the searing heat of skin on skin.

"This is all for you, Eli, every moment," Grey whispered as he brushed a soft kiss over Eli's lips. "Just let me take care of you, hmm?"

Grey lowered himself down, his hard body a welcome and comforting weight on Eli, the small but insistent rock of his hips pushing their iron-hard shafts together, dragging forwards then back, then forwards again, as all the time Grey peppered light kisses on his lips, on his cheeks, over the bridge of his nose, even on the tip of his nose.

Care... Let me take care of you... Whispered words that reached all the way into Eli's soul, into the very core of who he was, as he gave himself up to this man who seemed to know him more than he knew himself.

The rhythmic rock of their bodies picked up speed as Eli hitched his legs high and wrapped them tight around Grey's waist, pulling himself tighter into Grey's body, thrusting up hard. Grey grunted, as he lifted his head from where it had been buried in the crook of Eli's neck, and glared.

"I'm setting the pace, Eli." Grey pulled away, no more than a hair's breadth. His grin was smug and cocky, flirting with arrogance.

"You're killing me here," Eli breathed, bucking his

hips, but Grey moved back another tiny, barely there fraction of an inch, their hot and swollen dicks just out of
reach of one another.

Grey shook his head. "No, my little elf, not killing you.
I'm giving you what you need."

My little elf... Eli's heart rate spiked as a blazing heat
unfurled in the pit of his stomach, overwhelming him,
rolling through his blood in an irresistible wave. What he
needed? Yes, but didn't Grey need this too? One to give,
the other to receive; one to care, the other to be cared for.
As he stared up into Grey's beautiful, strong face, every
light in Eli blazed, illuminating all the dark and hidden
parts of him. And it had been Grey who'd flipped the
switch.

Eli rested his hand against Grey's cheek, feeling the
scrape of light stubble as Grey pushed into his palm. The
need to touch, the need to feel, the need for connection
was something both less and more than sex. It consumed
Eli, his heart leaping and flipping over and over as Grey's
eyes fluttered to a close. Yes, Eli needed this, he needed
them, but Grey did too.

Grey opened his eyes, his gaze dark and steady. Eli's
palm, still resting against Grey's cheek, slipped and fell to
his side.

There was no sound, not even the crackle and pop of
the fire; it was as though the whole room, the house, the
street and the city beyond the four walls, held its breath.

"Then let me take what you want to give me, Grey. Let
me take it all."

A handful of words, said on a soft breath, wrenched
open the dam.

Eli's gasp turned into a cry as Grey thrust hard against

him, his cock dragging over his own, sending an explosion of heat through every molecule of his body. Eli hitched his legs higher as he met Grey thrust for thrust. Chasing down the need for contact, connection, for skin on skin that was so much more than physical craving, their bodies writhed on the velvet-soft rug as rivulets of sweat ran over Eli's skin.

"Eli."

Everything was contained in that one murmur of his name. All the care, all the concern, everything to make it right and good for him. Eli's heart opened, laid bare it was an offering for this man who stared down at him and promised to keep him safe.

"Let me make everything good for you, Eli."

Grey's voice low and gruff as he wrapped his hand around both of their cocks, sliding from the base to the tip, to the base again. Grey's hips rode Eli as his palm rode their furnace-hot, crushed together shafts, as with his free hand he pushed his fingers, holding him still as he raided his mouth.

Eli was as hungry for the kiss as Grey. Urgent hunger consumed Eli, demanding all the kisses and more as he rocked his hips, pushing his burning, aching cock through the tight tunnel of Grey's fist, wet and slippery with their combined juices.

Desperation mounted in Eli. Desperation to come. Desperation to hold back. Desperation to let this perfect moment with this perfect man last forever. He needed more, needed to get closer to Grey, needed to crawl under his skin, needed to feel their release, the release that was mounting for both of them as their hard and relentless rhythm began to stutter.

Slipping a hand between their sweat-soaked bodies, Eli's palm joined Grey's wrapped around their squeezed together cocks. Grey arched back, just a little, just enough for Eli to gaze in open mouthed wonder at the tunnel their hands made, at the red, swollen, slick heads of their shafts, pumping into and out of their fists, jacking harder and faster.

Eli cried out as his balls tightened. "Oh fuck, oh fuck, fuck, fuck, Grey, I'm—"

"Let yourself go, little elf. I've got you, I won't let you fall."

Grey's words, heard through a fog of lust and longing, desire and need, and so much more his numb brain couldn't grasp, were the push that sent him tumbling over the edge.

Eli's body stiffened and stilled as his orgasm raced through and burst from him, as streams of creamy cum shot from him, hitting his stomach, his chest, flooding both their hands. Grey's shouted out curse sliced through the room before the first wave of Eli's climax had finished thundering through him, as Grey's hips shuddered and stuttered as he came, his release mixing and melding with Eli's own.

Grey collapsed on top of Eli, his breath hot and ragged on Eli's neck. With their chests pressed close, their hearts hammered as one.

"Gr—" It was as far as Eli got, as Grey stopped him with a kiss. Eli closed his eyes, his arms snaking around Grey's damp body, holding him tight, holding him close, welcoming his weight, as their hearts beat in a perfect, steady rhythm.

CHAPTER NINETEEN

Grey rolled onto his back and turned his head to gaze at Eli.

His little elf was staring up at the ceiling, his chest rising and falling. Like his own, Eli's body glistened under the lights cast by the dying fire and from the soft lamplight. With his bruised, puffy lips and wide, glazed eyes, Eli looked thunderstruck. He also looked sated and fucked, but more than that, with his loose limbs and the soft flush washing over his skin, he looked content.

A sudden thrill, smug and swaggering, ripped through Grey. *He'd* done this to Eli, *him*. Because he'd given Eli exactly what he'd needed, whether Eli had realised it or not.

Grey's heart clenched… Hadn't it been everything he'd needed, too?

My little elf…

"Grey?"

Eli's quiet voice sounded as though it was it was

coming from miles away. But it wasn't its faintness that caused concern to ripple through Grey, it was the edge of worry tinging Eli's voice. Grey frowned; whatever was wrong, it was for him to put right.

"Hello." Grey smiled and his heart almost burst through his ribcage when Eli smiled back, gazing at him through soft eyes.

"That was…" Eli's brow puckered slightly, and Grey studied him as Eli tried to put the pieces together of what had happened, which had been so much more than sex. "That… It…"

"Was amazing and incredible? Confirmation I am indeed a fully certificated sex god?"

Eli blinked at him before laughing, and Grey joined in, glad to blow away the charged air that had settled around them. For now, in this moment, all Grey wanted was to make what came next easy and light, with no place for doubts.

"Oh, it was okay. I suppose. Or maybe quite nice." Eli's face was deadpan but the twinkle in his incredible eyes was unmistakeable. Eli scooted in and wrapped himself around Grey.

Grey's heart rate spiked as Eli nuzzled in close, anchoring himself against him.

"This is nice," Eli murmured.

It was, a thousand times and more. Grey slipped his arm around Eli, who edged closer as though seeking warmth and shelter from a world that was cold and hostile.

"We should have a shower 'cause we're a mess." Eli chuckled, his breath soft against Grey's skin and sending waves of warmth through his blood.

"No rush. Here, just like this is good."

"Hmm, nice here, so nice…" Eli's words dissolved into a fuzzy, incoherent mumble before his breathing settled into an even in-out, in-out, as he fell asleep in Grey's arms.

Grey drifted his hands through Eli's dark, silky hair, a warm smile sweeping through his body when he was rewarded with a sigh. Even in his sleep, Eli craved to be cared for, all the bright and breezy front he put on to face the world stripped and thrown away.

As Eli slept soundly in his arms, Grey had never been more alert and awake. And alive, as a light had been switched back on in his life, melting away the gloomy shadows cast by the failure of his marriage. And it had all been because of his little elf, asleep in his arms. In a matter of days, just scant days, his world had changed and if he knew one thing, it was that he could never go back to that cold, sterile place that had been his existence before events had thrust this stunning man into his path.

In his arms, Eli shifted, and Grey gazed down. His heart melted at the sight of the younger man nestled hard against him, his arm thrown across Grey's chest as though afraid Grey might try and escape. Grey inclined his head, the impulse too great to resist even if he'd wanted to, to plant a soft and tender kiss on the top of Eli's head, his heart soaring as Eli sighed in response.

Grey closed his eyes and let himself sink into the moment, letting the warmth of the room and the warmth of the man in his arms ease him into sleep. He should sweep Eli up in his arms and carry him off to bed, but he didn't want to move or think any more, as he began to fall deeper and deeper…

Grey's eyes shot open, wide awake and brain on high alert, as he jerked up to sitting. Eli had fallen out of his arms and was curled up in a ball, one hand low behind his back, his face crunched up in pain.

"Eli? What's wrong?"

"Nothing, or not now your cock's only a lick away from my mouth. Ouch!" Eli's face scrunched some more.

Grey looked down at his dick. Like Grey, it was waking up after his nap.

"My lower back's a bit stiff, I think it's where I took the brunt of the fall earlier. It's nothing." Eli offered up a watery smile.

"Let me have a look."

"No, it's okay. But perhaps I should be in bed, somewhere a bit softer than the floor."

"I said, let me look." Grey's voice was calm, steady and steely, the voice he used for difficult clients. And as for going to bed, Eli would be slipping between the sheets of *his* bed tonight.

Eli turned onto his stomach, all argument shelved.

Grey winced. Just above the cleft of Eli's arse cheeks, a large bruise had formed, spreading out like a flooded lake. Anger began to fight its way out of Grey, and he clenched his teeth together hard.

Anger at himself.

How could he have not noticed? But he knew. He'd been too wrapped up in his own need for Eli when all that should have mattered was what Eli had needed.

He should have insisted on taking Eli to A&E earlier. He'd fallen hard, he'd been shocked and shaking, and had needed to be checked over by a doctor, despite his protestations. Grey sucked in a deep breath and threw a glance up at the ceiling. He should have listened harder to his instincts, and damn well taken matters into his own hands.

"It's just bruised, and it's stiffened up a bit." Eli mumbled. On his front, his face was buried into his crossed over arms. He lifted his head and looked up. "I've not damaged it, which I think we've proved, so no I don't need to go to A&E because I know what you're thinking."

"I still—"

"No. If I'd hurt myself beyond a few bruises I'd have known. Grey, stop scowling at me. I'm a wuss, okay? If I stub my toe, I run howling for the doctor. Like I said before, I'd just be told to take ibuprofen."

The tension holding Grey's shoulders relaxed. Eli was right, he knew he was, but it still didn't stop him from wanting to bundle Eli up in his arms and carry him off to hospital.

"Okay, you win," he huffed, "but let me take a closer look."

Gently, so, so, gently, Grey felt the bruise, checking for any signs of swelling or broken skin. Without thought, and on instinct alone, Grey placed a soft kiss on the dark patch. Under his lips, Eli shivered and sighed.

"That's nice, better than all the pain killers in the world, but talking of which…"

"Come on." Grey leapt to his feet and helped Eli to his, holding him tight when Eli winced. "I can carry you upstairs." He'd do it easily and willingly, but Eli shook his head.

"I'm fine. Honest. A shower, because well…" He looked down at his cum-splattered stomach.

They were both a mess. The thought of a long hot

shower with Eli was waking his dick up, but it wasn't what Eli needed right now.

"Sure. And then I'm putting you to bed." *My bed.*

Eli nodded, his face wreathed in a soft smile as though he'd heard Grey's silent words.

CHAPTER TWENTY

Grey peeled open his eyes and blinked into the bright light flooding the bedroom. The partially open curtains revealed a blue sky with not a snow cloud to be seen. His limbs were floppy and relaxed, the tension that had been the backdrop to his daily life for months on end all melted away to nothing. Life felt good, the days and weeks and months which lay ahead of him were as clear and bright as the blue winter sky. Gazing down at the reason for his new found optimism, a soft smile lifted his lips that could, maybe, be called sappy. But he had a lot to be sappy about.

Curled into Grey's side, Eli had slung one leg over Grey. Eli's lips puffed open, then closed, and opened again with each even breath. Grey couldn't pull his gaze away. With his dark auburn hair messy and ruffled, and the hint of scruff shadowing his jaw, Eli was stunning. There was no other word, or not unless gorgeous, beautiful and adorable were added into the mix to make the complete and perfect whole.

Eli shifted, his morning wood pressing into Grey's

thigh. A spear of desire shot through Grey, and his own dick, still a little sleepy, perked into life as his thoughts turned to breakfast which didn't include tea and toast. Eli murmured in his sleep, the words soft and smudged, and Grey bit down on the groan as his dick begged for attention. Eli shifted again, releasing his hold on Grey, who slipped from the bed. He stared down at his dick, flushed and pulsing, the head slick with pre-cum, primed and ready for action. He curled his palm around himself, drawing in a sharp breath as his whole body convulsed in a nerve tingling shiver. Breakfast, of the most mouth watering and delicious kind which would leave them sated... But maybe not this morning, as he padded to the en-suite leaving Eli to sleep.

"Morning."

Grey looked up from his laptop, which he'd set up on the kitchen table. Eli stood in the doorway, dressed in jeans and the soft dark green jumper, one of the two Grey had insisted they buy. He shuffled from foot to foot as though unsure, doubting his welcome on the morning after the night before.

No way was Grey going to leave Eli wondering.

"Hey, you." Grey smiled, but that wasn't hard to do when Eli was around. "How's the bruise?"

Eli came and sat down at the table. "Not too bad, considering. It received some very special TLC last night." Eli glanced away as two deep red patches coloured his cheeks, but he was smiling and that was all that mattered.

"Nothing wrong with TLC, Eli." Grey's heart banged

against his ribs. He had all the TLC in the world to give to the adorable, gorgeous man who needed it more than he knew.

"No, there isn't… Sometimes it's nice to just…" Eli frowned, biting down on his lower lip as he struggled to put his thoughts into words.

I can give you all the TLC you want, Eli…

The idea, that had hooked itself into Grey and refused to let go, had taken shape in little more than an hour. The words tingling on his tongue were madness, and an outrage to his ordered, logical brain. But as Grey's gaze followed Eli as he moved across the kitchen and flicked the switch on the kettle as though he did it every day, it wasn't his rational brain that had made its wants known loud and clear.

Grey closed down his laptop, pushed it aside, and glanced out through the glass doors leading into the garden. There had been another heavy load of snow dumped overnight, and it glittered and glimmered under the bright winter sun, making the world feel pristine and new. They had the whole day in front of them, a day that had the power to make their lives just as pristine and new, too.

Back at the table, Eli took a sip of tea and sighed. "The first cuppa of the day. Pure bliss."

"It's even better when somebody else makes it. Do you want breakfast?"

"I can cook for us, I'm more than happy to. There's bacon and eggs in the fridge." Eli jumped up, coming to an abrupt halt when Grey spoke.

"No, that's not what I mean. Let's go out. There's a place nearby, a deli with a café. You'll like it."

"That sounds lovely." Eli cocked his head to the side, his face thoughtful. "When I'm sorted in the New Year, I'm going to treat you to dinner. It'll all be on me. As long as it's Nando's."

"Nando's?" Grey raised a brow.

"Yep, you can't go wrong with spicy chicken and chips." Eli laughed. "But I'm serious. Okay?"

Grey smiled, but said nothing. Eli raced from the room, his tea forgotten, the thump of his feet on the stairs no match for the thump in Grey's heart.

With two days to go before Christmas Day, Lulu's Café and Deli was doing brisk business, everybody letting somebody else take the strain of cooking in the final run-up to the big day.

"This is great." Settling into his seat, Eli's face lit up as he looked around the café.

A converted chapel, the café's lofty ceiling was hung with reflective baubles which reminded Grey of mirrored disco balls. Lulu's had taken the order to deck the halls with boughs of holly to its literal extreme, as wreaths of winter greenery seemed to hang from every available piece of wall space. A large, bushy Christmas tree dominated one corner, dripping Santas and snowmen ornaments, silver stars, and red and green bows. Winding its way all around the tree, a rope of clear bright white lights gently twinkled. A shaft of sunlight burst through the stained glass window high above, bathing everything and all in jewel bright colour.

Eli picked up one of the menus from the table, and

Grey watched as Eli's eyes widened; he knew exactly what was going through Eli's mind as he scanned the choices on offer. The area was wealthy, and Lulu's catered exclusively to those who could pay the price without a second thought.

"I'll have poached egg on toast, please."

The plainest, cheapest thing on the menu.

Grey leaned across and lowered his voice, his words for Eli alone.

"Poached egg on toast is absolutely not a breakfast fit for the festive season. You've saved me from a dull Christmas on my own, with only Trevor's dubious company. I'm going for salmon and scrambled eggs, and a huge pile of sourdough toast, so—"

"What can I get for you today, guys?" A waitress bounded up to them, wearing reindeer deely boppers and Santa earrings. She smiled down at them, her stylus poised above the tablet she held, ready to take their order.

Grey raised his brow at Eli, who hesitated for a moment before he answered.

"Same as you. Thank you."

Grey gave the waitress their order. "And a couple of Buck's Fizz," he added, before she raced off.

Eli fiddled with the salt and pepper pots, not meeting Grey's eye. He was anxious and awkward and Grey wanted to put an immediate stop to it.

"Eli? Tell me what's up all of a sudden."

Eli's shoulders slumped as he let go of a small puff of air.

"I know how stupid it must sound, given everything you've done for me — when you never had to, despite what you think — but the prices in here, they're astronom-ical. The full English breakfast, it costs more than my

149

entire weekly lunch budget for work. I suppose it just brought into focus that once Christmas is over and we hit 1st January, I'll just be back to square one again."

Grey studied Eli across the small table. The noise and chatter, the chink of knives and forks on plates, and the carols playing in the background, faded away to nothing. Eli was proud. Proud of the way he was working towards his ambition, proud of the way he was doing it with nobody to back him up, and he had every reason to be so. Yet life had conspired to pull the rug from under his feet; he was falling and needed help to stand. He just needed to be persuaded of that.

Grey wanted nothing more than to sweep away the worried frown creasing Eli's brow, and to make those gorgeous lips of his smile once more. Grey took a deep breath, ready to lay before Eli the plan that had formed, all its pieces fitting together and snapping into place like a jigsaw puzzle.

"Two Buck's Fizz." The smiley waitress returned with flutes of the joyful, celebratory cocktail, its rich bright orange a burst of the summer sun which waited just beyond the horizon.

"Happy Christmas, Eli." Grey raised his glass, and Eli smiled as he did the same, the worry that had shadowed his face melting away.

"It is, thanks to you."

They chinked glasses. Eli sighed as he sipped on his drink.

"Hmm, lovely. I think I could start every day with one of these, although I don't think my liver would thank me for it."

"Daily indulgence is good for the soul. Maybe not alcohol based, though."

Eli tilted his head. "Yeah? What kind of indulgence do you have in mind?"

Eli's smile turned darker as he narrowed his eyes, both his question and his questioning gaze sending heat to Grey's dick, waking it up as it pushed against the prison of his jeans. It was all Grey could do to stop himself from lunging across the table and dragging Eli into to his arms to show him exactly the kind of indulgence he meant, the kind they could have morning, noon, and night, and all the times in-between. Instead, he took a sip of the drink he could barely taste, giving himself time to take a breath.

"Those that make you feel good."

Eli snorted. "I know what makes me feel good."

Grey sipped his drink, not taking his eyes from Eli. Did Eli know? Really, truly, deeply know? Grey wasn't so sure. Eli was talking about sex, but it was only one piece of the picture. Grey leaned forward, just a little, lessening the space between them, making their own little private island in the sea of festive revellers.

"What about waking up to soft kisses, or falling asleep in another's arms? Being wrapped up in a warm, protective blanket when you're cold, or being giving your favourite foods to eat when you're feeling low? Or having all your worries and concerns lifted from your shoulders and taken care of? Having another to carry your weight and hold you up, giving you all and every support you need when life feels like it's too much? Do those things make you feel good, Eli?"

The bustle of the crowded café, the chatter, the laughter, the Christmas music, it all died away to nothing. The warm air around them was charged, electrified, crackling. Grey's heart beat a hard, steady rhythm, its thump reverberating in every part of him as he gazed at Eli, waiting for him to answer not only Grey's questions, but his own.

Eli nodded, slow and small. "I—I've never had those things. Not since I was little, but I'm kind of guessing you're not talking about then." Eli dipped his head and gazed down at his glass, turning it by the long, slim stem. "But I know I'd like them, and to not have this feeling all the time that I'm pushing a boulder up a mountain where the summit is always just out of reach. I—I think that's what would really make me feel good."

Eli slumped back in his seat as though his confession had knocked the wind from him. His brow creased, as though he were working out a problem that had always been foggy and out of focus, but was now turning sharper and clearer.

The clamour of the café rushed back in, as the waitress returned bearing a tray with their orders. Neither said anything as they gave their attention to the food in front of them, but Grey cast Eli surreptitious glances. He could fulfil all those barely acknowledged needs for Eli, the need and desire to be cared for as much as he had the need and desire to care.

"Good?" Grey nodded to Eli's breakfast.

"It's great. Salmon and scrambled eggs is officially my favourite. I wonder if they'd work on jacket potatoes?" Eli laughed before he bit down on a piece of crunchy sourdough toast, butter smearing his lips.

The tip of his tongue glided along his lower lip, sweeping up the melted butter. Grey's cock once more pushed against its confinement. He itched to flee the café and get Eli home, to slam the door on the world so he could take care of Eli in all the ways he never knew he needed. He drew in a deep breath as, instead, he applied himself to his breakfast, catching the bubbly waitress for two more Bucks Fizz.

"Why, Mr. Gillespie, are you trying to get me drunk?" Eli said, with a laugh, as the waitress rushed off with the order. "You really are a wicked, wicked man."

"Oh, you have no idea how wicked I can be, little elf."

Eli's lips formed a small *O,* and his eyes widened, two inky pools, their divergent colours no more than thin outer rims around their irises.

"You could never be—"

"Your drink, guys, and a little sweet treat on the house."

The waitress set down the drinks, alongside two mini mince pies, bestowing a bright and increasingly frantic smile before she bustled away.

Grey pushed his mince pie towards Eli, who smiled in delight.

"You really know the way to a boy's heart." Eli bit into the tiny pie, and sighed.

Easy, companionable silence settled around them, a small island of calm in the hectic, noisy café that seemed to be growing busier by the second.

"Penny for them? You seem miles away."

Across the table, Eli was looking at him, his head tilted to the side. Most of his drink was gone, whereas Grey had barely touched his. Taking a steadying breath, Grey leaned forward, ready to lay out the idea that had formed earlier, now a fully considered, picked over proposal.

"This friend you mentioned, the one who'll be able to put you up in a couple of months—"

"Rufus. What about him?"

"How much do you want to rent a room from him?"

Eli wrinkled his nose. "Not very much, to be honest. I like him, he's a decent guy, but it'll be a pig getting into work from his place. But I don't have a lot of options. I'll just have to sit tight at Benny's and carry on fouling his little love nest until I've got myself sorted with Rufus."

"You don't have to do any of that."

"What do you mean?" Eli's brow furrowed in question. "I—"

"Your bill, guys."

The waitress appeared, armed with a card machine. She was still smiling, but it was starting to look like a grimace. Grey glanced around, and he couldn't blame her. A queue had formed outside, and was snaking along the road. The place was heaving, and what Grey wanted to say to Eli needed to be said privately.

He settled the bill, left the waitress a large tip, and moments later he and Eli were outside on the snowy street.

"What were you going to say, before we got turfed out?"

"Let's wait until we get home."

Home was only a few streets away. They slipped and slid on the compacted snow, Eli holding him and stopping him from falling just as much as Grey did the same for Eli.

"We haven't seen the last of the bad weather, have we?" Eli tilted his face to the sky, and Grey followed the direction of his gaze.

The earlier blue had gone, replaced by bulging clouds tinged with yellow. There was more snow to come, and it'd be coming soon. Grey smiled to himself. It could snow all it liked, it didn't matter, because he and Eli were going to be tucked away in the warm, with the door closed on the rest of the world.

Back at the house, it didn't take Grey long to get the fire going, and soon the grate was filled with dancing flames.

"So what were you going to say to me, in the café? You're being very secretive." Eli, curled up on the sofa, smiled up at Grey.

"It's an idea I have, which I need you to think seriously about." *But not think too long...* "Just hear me out, okay?"

Eli nodded as Grey sat next to him.

"Your current position, regarding your living situation, is unstable."

Eli barked out a rough laugh. "You can say that again. Sorry, go on."

"There's nothing to stop Benny from telling you to leave when he gets back; any rights you may have as a lodger are so minimal they're non-existent. You have somebody you'll be able to share with but not immediately. Unless you find somebody to let you have their sofa, there's a good chance you could be homeless for a period of time. That's your situation, but it doesn't need to be that way."

Eli shook his head. "Benny wants me gone, but he wouldn't throw me out on the street. I'm sure he wouldn't. He knows I've got Rufus as a back up plan. It'll be awkward but I can hack it for a few weeks. I think." Eli grimaced.

"Why try and hack it at all, when you don't need to? I said none of it needs to happen and I mean it."

Grey gazed at Eli, willing him to understand, willing him to join the dots and make the connection to what he was saying.

"Of course I'm going to have to put up with it. With all of it. I know what my situation is. It's pretty crappy but I guess it could be a lot worse, and I just have to keep reminding myself of that. I was hoping I could forget about it at least for a few days."

Grey took Eli's hands in his own, his thumbs sliding backwards and forwards across Eli's knuckles.

"I can change your situation, Eli, and I can do it now. I can make everything that's stressing you out and holding you back go away."

I can take care of you, I can protect you from all the crap that's being slung your way...

"But how? I don't understand."

"Don't you? Remember what I said in the café, about feeling good? How having somebody by your side who could take the worry and pressure away when it's all feeling like too much and is pulling you down? I can do that for you, Eli. I can make it all disappear."

Eli blinked. His mouth parted, as though he were about to say something, but he closed it as if unsure what to say, what to ask. Confusion knit Eli's brow, confusion Grey wished only to smooth away.

"You can stay here, with me, for as long as you want or need. Honestly, it'd be good not to come home to an empty house. Think about it: not having to wonder if Benny's going to chuck you and your belongings out on the street; not having to beg for somebody's sofa until Rufus gets back to the UK; not having to try and find expensive short term accommodation which'll blow your savings out of the water; not having to throw it all in and go to your mum and dad. If you stay here, in this house that's got more rooms than it has a right to, all that worry and all those problems will cease to exist."

Eli's big, beautiful eyes widened. "Why would you do that for me? I don't understand."

Because you need somebody to lean on, because you need help, because you need warmth and care against a world that's treating you with coldness and indifference…

The words danced on his tongue, eager to be said, but instead Grey paused, taking a moment to answer.

"Because you need help, and I'm in a position to give it. And I want to. Eli, I can see that you try hard and are willing to work to achieve what you want. I admire that, I admire it so much, and I don't want to see it all whipped away from you due to no fault of your own. Why let the world batter and bruise you when I can give you the shelter you need?"

Shelter, and so much more…

"It's… tempting. But I still don't understand."

"Like I say, it's because I can. And because I want to. I know what I'm offering, Eli. I'm not a man who makes rash decisions, about anything."

Eli looked down, at their joined together hands.

"This beautiful house in this area," Eli said quietly. "Hampstead, it's one of the priciest parts of London. There's no way I could afford to pay you anything like the market rate for rent." He glanced up, a rueful smile on his lips.

"I don't want or need rent. Yes, this house is beautiful, but it's also been bloody cold and lonely. Until some crazy little elf walked in. That alone is the only *rent* I want."

"Well, I guess I did look kind of cute as an elf."

"I guess you did, kind of."

Eli gave a small, shy smile. "I'd... I'd like that, until I get back on my feet properly. They do feel like they've been kicked out from under me recently, I've got to admit. But I want to pull my weight." Eli met Grey's eyes, pride and determination shining from him. "I'll do the cooking. And the housework."

"Cooking I'll say yes to, but not the housework. You're not going to be here as some kind of skivvy. I've got a cleaner who comes in a couple of times a week."

"I'll walk Trevor each day."

Grey laughed. "Good luck with that. He's a lazy little sod."

"Then what can I do?"

"What you like and what you're good at."

Grey started as Eli pulled his hands free, and jumped into his lap, straddling him in an instant. Rolling his body forward, Eli brought his mouth to Grey's ear.

"I know what I like and what I'm good at."

Grey shivered as Eli sucked his earlobe into his mouth.

"I meant making pizzas... jacket potatoes... weird toppings..."

Eli chuckled. "Oh, I think I can leave the... weird toppings... to you, Mr. Gillespie."

Everything and anything Grey wanted to say dissolved as Eli's kiss melted him. Their sighs and moans filled every corner of the room, as tongues slid over tongues as each delved deeper. Grey's hands clamped themselves to either side of Eli's hips, which had began a slow roll, with each wave pressing Eli's erection against his own.

Eli slid from Grey's lap, coming to a kneel on the floor

between Grey's splayed legs. The ache in Grey's cock was pushing into pain, the press against the zip on his jeans growing ever more insistent. Grey's heart catapulted when Eli pressed and rubbed his face into the heat between his legs.

"Eli, you don't have to... This isn't about... It was never about..." But Grey's incoherent thoughts broke up and fell away as Eli unbuckled and unzipped him, and freed his needy, desperate cock.

Between Grey's legs, Eli sat back and looked up. His eyes were dark with desire, his lips puffy and bruised, his hair a mussed up mess. Grey's cute little elf had morphed into a dark and dirty angel.

"I know I don't. But I want to. I want to very, very much, Mr. Gillespie."

Eli dipped his head and took him deep into his mouth, leaving Grey to release a long and shuddering moan as he tumbled into the abyss.

CHAPTER TWENTY-ONE

Eli lay on the sofa with Trevor snuggled up beside him, and eyed the mince pies. Thank goodness for Grey's tooth, as sweet as his own, because there were boxes and boxes of them.

"Hmm, lovely." Eli groaned as he bit into one. "No! Bad Trevor!"

He whipped away the half eaten little sweet treat, just in time to stop Trevor snatching it away, knowing just a taste of the gooey vine fruit filling would make the little dog very ill.

"These are for two legged animals, not four. I'll get you a Crunchie Snax in a minute. All right, be like that," Eli said as Trevor huffed — Eli was sure he huffed — and slid from the sofa, skulking off into the corner of the room where he turned his back on Eli.

It was the perfect Christmas Eve. Or it would have been perfect, if Grey were with him rather than locked away in his office. *Last time, I promise*, Grey had mouthed as he took the call before he'd disappeared. Eli pushed himself deeper into the cushions. It was the nature of Grey's high powered job, he supposed, but Grey had promised it would be the last work call he took, and Eli believed him.

Eli stared into the flames licking at the logs in the grate, and let his mind drift.

Were he and Grey becoming a couple? Eli wasn't sure, but weren't all the signs there? Wasn't it only a question of time? He narrowed his eyes as he sought to find the word that described them. *Complemented.* Yes, that was it, they complemented each other. But wasn't it more than that? Weren't they — simpático? Eli scrunched up his nose at the word Benny had started using to describe his relationship with the odious Lenny. But, yeah, simpático... Eli got it, for the first time he really got it.

Eli glanced at his watch. Midmorning, Grey had been gone just over an hour; perhaps a coffee would be welcome.

Pushing himself up, he didn't get much further than a few steps when the door bell rang. With Grey shut away in his office, Eli open the door.

"Hello," the guy standing on the doorstep said, his eyes widening in surprise before he smiled. "I'm looking for Grey."

Eli said nothing. His stomach plummeted and he gripped the edge of the door. The smile was dazzling, as it would be from a man who was beautiful enough to have once been a model, a man Eli had seen looking out from an arty black and white wedding photograph. The man who'd lived in this house, with Grey. The man who'd shared his bed. The man who'd been his husband.

Peter Carr, the former Mr. Peter Gillespie.

"Are you okay? You look very pale."

Peter's voice was laced with concern, breaking through the high pitched whine screaming in Eli's head.

What the hell was Grey's ex-husband doing here, on Christmas Eve?

Eli nodded. "Yeah, he is," he croaked, forcing the words out through frozen lips. "But he's working. In his office. A call, earlier. Some crisis." Eli still clutched the door, the only thing keeping him upright on his wobbly legs.

"Ah, yes. Nothing's changed, then. Perhaps I could come in? It's getting rather chilly standing here." Peter looked up at the sky from which a fresh fall of snow was just starting.

"Er, yes. Of course. He should be finishing now. I'll get him." Eli jumped back, allowing Peter in.

Peter shook his head. "No, I'll wait for a bit. I know how he is when he's buried away in his office; he won't appreciate being disturbed, especially if there's a crisis on." Peter gave a wry smile.

Eli's stomach clenched hard. Of course Peter would know, because he was the former Mr. Gillespie, the man who knew Grey inside out.

"I'll, erm, make some coffee if you'd like?" Eli mumbled.

"Yes, please. Black, no sugar."

Peter dragged off his woolly hat, shaking out a mass of dark, glossy curls and raking his fingers through it. It was longer than in the wedding photo, more wild.

"I'll be in the living room. I know where it is." Peter laughed.

Eli dashed to the kitchen, leaving Peter to make his

way through the house that had been his not so very long ago. He switched on the kettle — no way was he making a fancy coffee, Peter could have instant. Eli rummaged in the draw for a spoon, which his clumsy fingers dropped. Pouring boiling water into the mug too quickly, a droplet splashed up at him, and he swore long and hard.

"Fuck. Fuck, shit, shitty shitty fuck, *shit!*"

Eli snorted; his granddad would have been proud of how blue he'd turned the air.

Peter. Grey's ex. The man who'd turned Grey's life upside down. Here, now, in the living room, and waiting for Grey. Eli rubbed his hands down his face. Taking a deep breath, he tried and failed to stick a smile on his face.

With the coffee shaking in one hand, Eli pushed the living room door open with his other. Peter was on his knees in front of the fire, grinning down at Trevor who was wriggling around on his back, legs akimbo as Peter rubbed his belly.

Little tart…

"I miss this funny old thing so much." Peter looked up at Eli and smiled.

Christ, he needed sunglasses to protect his sight from the dazzle. No wonder Grey had fallen for him. Eli's heart tumbled. Now the initial shock of Peter's arrival had passed, all he felt was flat and dejected.

Peter was stunning, there was no other word. A thick mass of dark shiny hair, hazel eyes sparkling green and gold, and cheekbones that were sharp enough to cut through stone. In the arty black and white wedding photo he'd been striking, his good looks undeniable, but it was a pale and thin version of the real life flesh and blood man.

Eli put the drink down on the coffee table and shuffled

from foot to foot, unsure whether to stay or go. Was Peter wondering who he was? Eli didn't owe the guy any explanation, Peter wasn't married to Grey any more, but—

"I'm Eli."

Peter got up from his knees with effortless ease. Now he was no longer bundled up in his coat, his dark chinos and plain black jumper moulded themselves to his slim, lithe body.

"Thank you for the coffee, Eli."

Peter didn't so much sit down on the sofa, as glide down. He picked up the drink and took a small and delicate sip, his sparkling curious gaze locked on Eli.

"As I think you may be aware, I'm Peter. Grey's ex-husband?" The upwards inflection in his voice made the statement into a question. Eli nodded. "I wasn't aware Grey had met anybody. Not that it's my business of course, or not any more, although for nearly fifteen years..." Peter shrugged.

Fifteen years? Peter's words were a punch to Eli's stomach. Why had he never asked Grey how long he and Peter...? Eli felt a total, utter fool. He hadn't even known Grey for fifteen days. His stomach went into free-fall

"So, you're a friend of Grey's? I telephoned, and he said he had somebody staying, but the line was bad. I'm guessing that somebody is you? So, how did the two of you meet?" A smile hovered over Peter's lips, before he covered his mouth with his hand, and laughed. "I'm sorry. Please, just tell me to butt out. I promise I won't be offended. Out and out nosiness is not my most attractive quality."

No, but you've got lots of other attractive qualities *to compensate...* Eli's spirits dropped further. He didn't blame Peter — the name all but stuck in his throat — for being curious. The man he'd seen in the photo, the man he'd told himself he would never meet and would hate if he did. His stomach bit down on itself, because neither of those things was turning out to be true.

Peter was friendly, polite, and calm. Eli wasn't quite so sure he'd be as sanguine if he'd turned up at the house that had once been his home only to find his former husband's boyfriend or lover hanging around. As Peter smiled at him over the rim of his coffee mug, Eli's less than certain certainties fled; he didn't know what he was to Grey.

"I'm sorry, Eli. Like I say, it's not my business."

"No, it's okay. We met at a party." Which was true, as far as it went. Peter didn't need to know about his stint as a slutty elf, attempting to nick Grey's coat, and hiding in the back of the Jag.

Peter's brows arched high, clear and genuine surprise on his face.

"A party? Well, that's not what I was expecting. Grey was never one for parties. He'd stand in the corner, clutching his drink with grim determination, and would drag us both home before midnight. Honestly, it was straight out of Cinderella." Peter laughed and shook his head. "Well, things seem to have changed in the last few months. But I'm glad, because he needed to be more social. There's more to life than working all the hours god sends."

A frown creased Peter's smooth brow as he took another sip of coffee, but it was gone in an instant and he smiled at Eli once more.

"Perhaps you wouldn't mind putting your head around the door for me? I just wanted to wish him Happy Christmas, and to give him this." Peter pulled his coat, which he'd lain over the back of the sofa, towards him and rummaged in the inside pocket. When he pulled his hand out, he held a parcel wrapped in plain brown paper. "It's a —oh, talk of the devil."

Peter's smile was brighter than the Saharan sun at midday as he turned towards the door. Eli followed his gaze to see Grey standing in the doorway, all his attention on Peter. Striding across, Grey wrapped Peter up in his arms.

"Hello, what are you doing here?" Grey said, this voice muffled as he buried his face in Peter's neck.

Checking up, seeing who your friend *is. You said he'd come round...*

Eli stepped back, just a bystander to he didn't know what.

"Hope you don't mind me calling in unexpected? I couldn't hear half of what you said the other—"

"Of course I don't."

Eli's heart tumbled as Grey smiled at Peter, his eyes for nobody other than the man he'd known and loved for fifteen years.

And still loved. Eli's fracturing heart shattered.

Unseen by either Peter or Grey, Eli slipped out of the living room and quietly closed the door behind him.

CHAPTER TWENTY-TWO

"Eli? Oh."

Grey pulled himself out of the hug. It was nothing more than friendly, no frisson for what had once been. Eli had gone, the door closed on himself and Peter.

"He's cute." Peter nodded towards the door, a smile floating on his lips, as he sat back down on the sofa. "He said you met at a party, which was a surprise."

"*He* is Eli, and yes we did."

Grey joined him. He had no intention of explaining the circumstances around his and Eli's meeting. What he was more interested in was why Peter, after months of no contact other than a disjointed call, was back at the house that had been his one-time home. Grey pressed his lips together, because wasn't it precisely because of the call he was here? He hadn't been joking when he'd told Eli that Peter had the gall to come round, but he hadn't truly expected it.

"Sorry. Yes, Eli. And as for the rest, it's mind your own

business." Peter laughed, but almost instantly he began to scratch the back of his neck.

Grey narrowed his eyes at the sign of nerves, nerves that in all the years he and Peter had been together had rarely manifested themselves. The last time they had was when Peter had told him he was leaving.

Grey didn't answer, but instead asked a question of his own.

"Why are you here, Peter? It's not that I'm not pleased to see you…" Grey wasn't so sure of that, but with some time behind them, and the sudden and brighter path his life had taken in recent days, he was inclined to feel generous towards his ex.

"There are a couple of reasons, including this." Peter picked up the plain wrapped parcel he'd dropped to the coffee table when Grey had come into the living room, and handed it across.

"A Christmas present?"

Peter shrugged. "Yes, and no. David, Jessica and I," he said, referring to his siblings, "have been clearing out Dad's place, getting ready to sell in the New Year. It was where I was phoning from, which was why the signal was so bad."

Grey took the proffered parcel. Peter's late father had lived in a remote and tiny village, close to the sea in Suffolk. Peter had always said it was like going back in time, and the sketchy phone signal seemed to agree.

"I didn't want to *not* wish you the best for the season, but when I found this it was the perfect reason to come and see you. That, and your mention of a friend, of course."

Grey said nothing as he pulled the paper loose. He wished Peter no ill will, but it had been him who'd wrecked their marriage — and now he wanted to nose around in his life, a life he was no longer a part of. The paper fell away from the package.

Ah...

Grey smiled despite the confusion of thoughts and emotions coursing through him. An copy of *Wind in The Willows*, an early edition but by no means a first, battered and beaten. He and the old man had discovered a shared enjoyment of the classic and timeless children's story.

"This could be valuable." Grey held it up and raised a brow. Peter shook his head.

"No. I had it valued. But I thought you might like it, seeing as you and Dad got on so well."

"We did. And thank you, I appreciate it."

They fell into silence. Peter carried on drinking his coffee, and Grey looked at his watch. He was finished with work for the day, and for Christmas, and he wanted to spend the time with Eli.

"Is that the signal for me to push off?" Peter smirked.

"Kind of, but you said there were a couple of reasons why you were here."

"I did, but the other doesn't seem to be quite as pressing any more." Peter put his mug down, and locked his gaze on Grey's. "I know you may not believe me, but I didn't like the idea of you spending Christmas alone. Especially," he said, his voice dropping, "this first Christmas. Oh, for god's sake, Grey, stop looking at me like that."

Grey stared at him, and shook his head.

"How should I look at you, then? After all, there was a very good reason for me, possibly, being on my own wouldn't you say?" Grey spat the words at Peter, who nodded and looked away. Grey's flash of anger subsided as quickly as it had flared. "Well, as you can see I won't be on my own." *Now you know, just go.*

If Peter picked up the unspoken message, he took no notice of it.

"And I'm glad that's the case. I really am. I saw Barney and Maxwell earlier in the week, and they said you'd declined an invite to theirs for Christmas."

Grey shuddered. "You really thought I'd want to spend it with them?"

Peter's lips twitched a smile. "They're lovely, if a little earnest."

"They also have an unhealthy addiction to tedious and very long board games. I stopped playing Trivial Pursuit years ago, and I don't intend to restart." Grey couldn't help but return Peter's smile.

"Okay, but I also know you refused other invites. And you'd never go to your brother's—"

"So what were you going to do? Suggest we spend Christmas together? Bit weird, wouldn't you say?"

"I just didn't like the thought of you being alone. We may no longer be together, Grey, but you'll always be important to me."

Grey exhaled a long breath. "I appreciate the sentiment. I think. But it's not needed because I'm not going to be..." It came to him in a blinding flash... He hadn't considered... Peter would be with David, or with Jessica, wouldn't he...? Was it Peter who...? "Are you going to be on your own?"

Peter shook his head, as a flush crept up his face. "No, I'm not. I, well I..." He scratched the back of his neck again. Grey waited for the words to stumble out. "I've met somebody."

Grey sat motionless as he stared at Peter. Of course he'd have met somebody. The man was witty, educated, interesting, and gorgeous, he was a man who turned heads as he walked into a room, a man whose smile, touch or kiss had left Grey panting and breathless, consumed with heat and need.

As Grey's eyes remained locked on Peter, he felt nothing.

"Anybody I know?" Just weeks earlier, days even, Peter's news would have devastated him, but now there was no more than a mild ripple of interest.

"No. I only met Crispin a couple of months ago." Peter looked up, and Grey read the words swimming in his eyes… *I never left you for another man… I never betrayed you…*

Grey believed the pleading he saw in Peter's eyes. The issue had never been about an interloper. It had been about them, or more about what he had wanted for him and Peter not being what Peter had wanted at all.

"I'm pleased for you. So who is this Crispy?"

"Crispin, not Crispy." Peter frowned. "He's a circus skills trainer, very well known in—"

Grey gawped before he burst into laughter. It was the last thing he'd expected to hear.

"Circus skills? What did he do to reel you in? Throw a custard tart in your face, or squirt water at you from a big plastic flower on his lapel?"

Peter glared at him. "I should have known you'd laugh. I'm sorry his profession isn't serious or buttoned up enough for you. Crispin's got his own well regarded academy, and he's been asked to help set up a school in

Mexico, in the New Year. He's going to be away for three months, and I'm going with him."

"I'm sorry, but — circus skills? Can somebody really make a living out of that?"

"I think—" Peter fell silent.

Grey swallowed the rest of his laughter. "You think what?"

Peter lowered his head. "All right, so it's not banking but that doesn't make it any less of a career choice, and for me that's a good thing. The world that comes with it, it's more me."

"More you than the stultifying, suffocating corporate world I was chained to — and by extension, you were too — is that what you're saying?"

The words were glass, tearing Grey's mouth to shreds. The bitterness, the pain, the anguish of who and what they'd been together tumbled down around him, as it all came flooding back. He didn't want to go back, not now, not ever, but it didn't stop Peter's words feeling like a scab had been pulled from a wet and weeping wound.

Grey jumped up from the sofa and turned away from Peter. He closed his eyes and drew in a long breath. All of that was gone, in the past, the signatures on the divorce papers confining it all to history.

A hand rested on his shoulder. Taking another deep breath, Grey turned around.

"Just be happy for me. Please?" Peter looked up at him with beseeching eyes.

Grey nodded. "I'm sorry. I shouldn't have bit like that. I am happy for you, if it's what you want. If Crispin is who you want."

"It is, and yes, he is. Tell me about Eli."

Grey jumped, Peter's words taking him aback.

Peter laughed. "Ohhh, have I made a dent in that cool, deadpan façade of yours? You're blushing, Grey, and you never blush."

"What do you want to know?" Grey asked, his voice gruff. But Peter was wrong. He hadn't made a dent in his cool, he'd kicked it out of sight.

"Everything, but I know you'll tell me sod all."

Correct...

"He's gorgeous. And those two-coloured eyes, simply stunning. But it was something else, really, that struck me. Despite his obvious shock at meeting me, he somehow looked very at home here, as though he fitted right in. And the goofy smile on your face when you walked into the living room — which was then ruined when you saw me — well, that told its own story."

Grey looked down, unable to hold Peter's assessing gaze.

"Well, I've never seen you lost for words. Or squirm. Must be love." Peter laughed softly, as he rubbed Grey's shoulder.

Love...

Was it? Grey didn't know what word to pin to what he was feeling for Eli. His cautious, logical brain told him it was too soon to be surrendering himself to all the stratospheric, soaring emotions that were wrapped up in that one little word, but... Wasn't that what he felt when he looked at Eli, when he wrapped his arms around him and held him tight? When he touched him, when he kissed him, when he made love to him?

"I... It's too soon to be thinking like that," Grey mumbled.

Peter shook his head, an indulgent smile on his lips.

"Love comes when it comes." He snorted. "That sounds a little smutty, but," he said, his voice and expression losing all levity, "there's no timetable. What you feel, and who you feel it for, can't be regulated and codified. Love doesn't confine itself to rules and regulations, Grey."

"I've only known him for—"

"Seconds, months, or years, it doesn't matter. When you know somebody is—"

"Like you and Crispin the Juggler?"

Peter tutted, not rising to the bait to turn the burning spotlight away from Grey.

"Yes, like me and Crispin. And like you and Eli. One thing I know about you, Grey, and that is you're not meant to be alone. You have too much to give, in here." Peter pressed his hand to Grey's heart. "If you truly believe you and he have a chance, for god's sake don't let it go. We may have run our course, but I'll always want the best for you. I'll always be here for you."

Grey wrapped his arms around the man he'd once loved with all his heart. The burning heat of that love had died away, never to be rekindled, leaving in its place the warmth of fondness and memories of a happier time which were now relegated to the past. Grey pulled back; resting his hands on either side of Peter's face, he placed a chaste kiss on his forehead.

"Happy Christmas, Peter. I mean it."

"You too, Grey. Say goodbye to Eli for me. What I've just said, think about it." Peter kissed his fingertips, before pressing them to Grey's lips. "There you go, sealed with a kiss. See me out, then go and find your cutie."

CHAPTER TWENTY-THREE

Closing the door on Grey and Peter, Eli felt sick. Grey's smile had been warm and bright as he'd spotted his ex-husband, both men having eyes for nobody but each other.

Eli leaned against the door, his legs shaking, as the murmur of their voices drifted through. He didn't want to hear, he really didn't, but... It wasn't Eli's finest hour, but he didn't care about that, or dignity, or any of the other arguments that should have sent him into the kitchen, or dining room, or anywhere that was far away from the living room where he'd left Grey and Peter smiling into each other's eyes.

Eli pressed his ear to the door. Good natured voices, and laughter. Eli's guts tightened. How could Grey sit and chat, and fucking well laugh with the man who'd walked out on him? They may have been divorced, but what did that have to do with how Grey still felt about the man he'd been with for...

Fifteen years.

Fuck. How could he compete with that? The men who

175

chatted and laughed on the other side of the door, the men who'd smiled at each other as though nobody else existed — okay, like *he* didn't exist — were still bound together by the bonds of a shared life and history the muffled laughter told him he didn't have. Eli stumbled away, unable to listen to any more.

In the kitchen, Eli collapsed into a chair at the table and let his head fall into his hands. He'd been duped, but he'd been duped by himself, because didn't Grey still—

Eli's heart crashed against his ribs, and he licked his dry lips. Closing his eyes, he took a deep breath because what was the use of denying it?

Grey still loved Peter.

So what that they were divorced? A scrap of paper didn't obliterate what Grey still felt for the man who'd been his everything. Eli gulped and his heart turned and twisted as it laughed at him. The way Grey had looked at Peter as though he were the only man in the world, Eli unnoticed on the sidelines as Grey had taken the man he still truly wanted, deep in his heart, into his arms.

"And they've only been divorced for six months." Eli's whispered words seemed to bounce off the kitchen walls, but there was nobody to hear them other than himself and a small dog who'd forgotten all about him as he'd surrendered himself to Peter, eager to show him he'd not been forgotten, that Peter was still loved. Just as Grey himself had done.

Who was he kidding? There was no great romance, no new beginning, no happy ever after. He snorted and shook his head. He'd wanted to believe so, so much he'd blinded himself to the reality of his position.

Grey was a good and decent man. Eli swallowed hard.

Oh, he wanted all that goodness and decency in his life, and all the care, protection and safety a man like Grey could give him. And he could have it, too, for a few days, a few weeks even — until he got himself sorted with a new place to live, until he got himself back on his feet. And then that lifeline Grey had offered would be severed, setting him adrift once more in the turbulent water that was his life. He and Grey were passing ships, it was all they ever were, and Eli had been a fool to believe otherwise.

It was time for him to find shelter in another harbour.

"What are you doing out here? It's freezing. And I didn't know you smoked."

Eli jumped, and swung around, so caught up in his torrid, turbulent thoughts he'd not heard the door from the kitchen open. Hunching against the cold on the icy patio, he looked down at the cigarette wedged between his fingers. The sudden, urgent need for a hit of nicotine had been all-consuming, and it hadn't taken long to creep out of the house to go to the shop on the corner. That had been half an hour ago, and the paper was burning low on his third ciggie.

"Yeah. I, erm, I've actually given up, but sometimes I get the craving. Filthy habit, though." He stubbed it out on the scrunched-up packet he pulled from the hip pocket of his jeans, and jammed the dog end inside.

"What's made you want to smoke again?"

Eli shrugged. "It just happens sometimes." *Like when I'm really, really, really stressed. Like when former husbands turn up out of the blue.* "I shouldn't have lit up, even in the garden."

"Eli, you can have whatever you want — except money for cigarettes."

Eli squirmed, and summoned up the courage to look Grey in the eye.

"I'm sorry. I saw your change jar in the kitchen... I shouldn't have pinched the cash."

Grey shrugged. "It's not the money. I just don't want you buying cigarettes."

And I don't want to see you look at Peter the way you did, but hey, you can't have everything in life.

"Come inside. I've finished work, and that's it until the New Year. Let's have lunch — perhaps jacket potatoes with some Eli Original toppings?" Grey smiled and arched his brows. Eli smiled back, even though it felt like the curve of his lips was held in place by thin and fragile threads.

They microwaved the potatoes then finished them off in the oven to crisp up. Baked beans and cheese were dumped on top, the perennial best seller.

Eli stared down at the meal he didn't want. Christ, somebody had to mention Peter, and it didn't look like it'd be Grey any time soon.

"He seemed nice. Peter, I mean." Eli attempted to smile across the table to Grey, but gave it up as a bad job.

"He is." Grey forked up some fluffy potato.

Eli mashed his beans down; he wasn't sure if he'd actually eaten anything.

"Did he ask you who I was?" Eli's breath baited as he waited for Grey to tell him.

Grey laughed quietly. "He was curious but I just told him what you'd already said, that we met at a party."

"He must have wondered about me, though? After all, this used to be his home."

Why am I asking this stuff? But Peter's sudden arrival was a scab Eli couldn't help but pick at.

Grey jumped up, and made for the sink where he filled two large glasses with water which he brought back to the table.

"We didn't really talk about who you are and how you've come to be here." Grey chugged down half the water in his glass.

Eli's shoulders twitched at Grey's clipped, brusque tone. Grey wasn't giving him that unnerving stare, but his face was closed off, his features unreadable.

We didn't really talk about who you are... Not talked about, as though he wasn't important enough to waste breath on.

Eli picked at the scab some more.

"Then what did you talk about? You seemed very pleased to see each other."

Grey took another gulp from his glass, almost emptying it, his gaze over the rim locked on Eli. Eli held it, resisting the urge to dive under the table like a cowed puppy.

"It was good to see him again. He was being nosy, just as I said he'd be, and he admitted as much. But he was concerned I'd be on my own over Christmas, and I know him well enough to know it was genuine. I've barely seen or heard from him since the divorce, and I suppose we've both been letting the dust settle. But, we were together for years, and most of that time was good."

Grey put his glass down with a hard thump, hard enough for Trevor to issue an admonishing bark from his pillow in the corner.

"He gave me a gift, a book that holds sentimental value. He also came to tell me he's met somebody. A circus skills trainer, of all things. Not convinced that's going to run the course, but then who am I to talk because the two of us didn't, either."

Grey scowled and stabbed at what was left of his potato before he pushed his plate away. He looked at Eli and smiled, but Eli didn't miss the shadows in Grey's eyes, dulling their vibrant blue. He looked fed-up, downcast and dejected; his ex-husband had found a new man and a new life and he didn't like it one little bit.

It's because you still love him…

What would Grey say if Peter asked for a second chance, to put the past behind them and start again? The packet of cigarettes burned in Eli's pocket, the urge to pull them out and light up every single one and suck all that poisonous smoke deep down into his lungs clawed at him.

Grey gathered up the plates, making no comment on Eli's untouched meal, his gaze settling for a moment on Eli before he turned away.

"Come on, it's Christmas Eve so let's watch some feel good films and gorge on mince pies."

Feel good films, an abundance of sweetness to disguise the bitterness of real life.

Eli nodded and forced a smile on his face as he got up and let Grey lead him into the living room.

CHAPTER TWENTY-FOUR

The coffee table was strewn not just with mince pies, but with little stollen bites and what remained of the box of artisan chocolates, plus a couple of glasses of egg nog. With the fire burning in the grate as the snow fell thick all over the city, it should have been the perfect easing into Christmas proper. But nothing felt right. Everything was skewed and off centre, the calm waters of the last few days now turbulent and raging.

Grey stared at the TV screen, seeing nothing, as he on autopilot he ate the sweet treats and sipped the heady winter drink, tasting nothing.

Peter's unannounced appearance had surprised Grey; it had been like bumping into an acquaintance he'd not seen for a while, somebody to pass the time with and wish them well before moving on. That in itself had been something of a revelation, a sure test that he and Peter were truly over. But, it had been what Peter had said about Eli, his little elf, that had rocked Grey to his core and had occupied every one of his thoughts since.

Grey gazed down at Eli, curled up next to him on the sofa. He'd fallen asleep, and Grey smiled. Eli, bright and breezy with a touch of sass and snark. It was all a mask, because he'd seen the man behind the disguise, stripped bare and vulnerable. And didn't he just want to wrap his arms around him and protect all that vulnerability against the knocks the world would inflict?

Grey's lips pressed into a hard line. Would inflict...? No, because hadn't the world already hit out at Eli? Grey drifted his fingers through Eli's dark, heavy hair and Eli sighed and pushed into his touch.

"You need looking after, little elf, you need somebody to take the weight and the burden when it gets too much."

Grey knew he'd been quiet over lunch. He'd been pre-occupied as he'd gone over Peter's visit, forensically dissecting it as he'd eaten without tasting, his motions automatic and pre-programmed, all the time coming back to what Peter had said, with his knowing smile, just as he'd come back to it over and over as he'd stared unseeing at the TV. *You're not meant to be alone, Grey. You have too much to give, in here... Love comes when it comes... There's not a timetable. What you feel, and who you feel it for, can't be regulated and codified.*

It must be love.

Grey scrubbed his hands down his face. Eli had found a way into his heart, pressing every single one of the buttons of who Grey was. They both had deep seated needs, one to care, the other to be cared for. But was that truly love?

Love comes when it comes.

Grey jumped and a shiver ran the length of his spine; he swung his head around, half expecting to see Peter behind him, looking down at him with his smile that knew the truth. In the corner Trevor jumped up and growled, his ears pulled back and twitching.

"It's okay, boy, it's okay," Grey said on a shaky breath. Trevor settled, and Grey looked down at Eli again, lying still and sleeping.

Grey resumed the gentle drift of his fingers through the hair of the man who had proved that, no, there was no timetable, regulation or rulebook.

Grey woke with a start. The TV was off and the room was in darkness, save for the last few embers from the fire and the faint glow leeching in from the street lamp. His heart thumped hard, his breath heavy in his lungs, and he sucked in deep to slow and steady his heart rate. Peering into the darkness, the space on the sofa next to him was empty.

Eli?" he called out, but his call went unanswered.

Grey pushed himself up, rolling his shoulders and easing out the tightness in his neck from slipping down the sofa in his sleep. He turned on the lamp next to him and peered at his watch, his eyes widening. *Six o'clock?* Afternoon had turned to early evening.

The living room door was ajar and Grey pulled it open, glancing into the corner where he'd last seen Trevor, but he too seemed to have disappeared.

"Eli? Where are you?" Grey called again, but like before there was no answer.

No Eli and no Trevor, so Eli must have woken up and taken the little dog out for a walk. Grey's lips quirked a smile. Trevor was the laziest dog alive, who didn't like snow even more than he didn't like the rain, or the sunshine, or doing anything more active than moving from one cushion to the next.

"Wish you'd woken me, though," Grey muttered to himself as he made his way to the kitchen.

A walk in the snow, on Christmas Eve, hand in hand and declarations of love… Grey's heart leapt in his chest, any idea about timetables ripped up and thrown to the wind. Maybe those declarations could be made on the rug, in front of the fire… once Eli got back with Trevor whining in his arms, because there was no way that dog would be walking anywhere.

Armed with a coffee, Grey started to make his way back to the living room, coming to a stop when a high pitched whimpering sounded from along the hallway, followed by frantic scratching.

"Trevor? What are you doing here?" Grey abandoned the coffee on the hallway table and rushed to the front door where Trevor was pawing, his whimpers filled with distress. "What's wrong, boy? Where's Eli?"

Grey scooped up the small dog, but Trevor wriggled and writhed so much Grey put him down before he fell from his arms. Grey called out again, knowing he'd receive nothing but silence. A shiver passed over him, and Grey wound his arms around his middle as realisation began to dawn.

Peter's sudden appearance and Eli, his usual lively self muted over lunch, the lunch he'd not touched. And him, pre-occupied as he mulled over his conversation with his ex-husband.

"Oh, shit."

Grey flew up the stairs, to the room Eli had stopped

184

sleeping in. He threw open the wardrobe door. All the clothes they'd bought together were still there, hanging up or neatly piled. A wave of relief flooded through him. Eli's clothes were there, so that meant… Grey looked down. No boots. And the coat, the old one of Grey's and way too big for Eli, the coat he wore because he wouldn't let Grey buy him one, because who wore a coat indoors? Boots and coat gone, and the silky fine woollen scarf, too.

Grey slammed the wardrobe door, the force of the slam causing it to swing open again. Grey grabbed hold of it, to keep himself upright on his trembling legs. Eli had gone, he'd left without hearing everything Grey wanted and needed to say to him, without hearing how much Grey loved him.

Beneath him, Grey's legs buckled and he sank to the floor.

Did Eli think that, deep down, he still wanted Peter, that he'd jump at a second chance with the man he'd spent so many years of his life with?

Eli was wrong, so damn wrong, and he needed to be put right. But first Grey had to find him.

Think.

Where would Eli go on Christmas Eve? His options were limited to the point of non-existent. Public transport, like the rest of the city, was closing down. No buses, no trains, no tube. The tube. The northern line, running straight from Hampstead to Stockwell and the little terraced house Eli was locked out of.

A couple of minutes later, dragging on his coat as he fled the house, slipping and sliding on the icy pavement, Grey jumped in his car. Flicking the ignition on, the heavy four wheeled drive rumbled into life and Grey pulled away from the kerb, cutting through the snow-bound road with ease. With his hands in a tight, white knuckled grip on the steering wheel, Grey headed for the tube station deter-mined to stop Eli from breaking in to a house miles and miles away, on a little south London street.

CHAPTER TWENTY-FIVE

"No. No, no, *no*."

Eli's hands clutched at the metal railings, chained and locked, barring his way into the tube station.

"Sorry, mate. You're too late. Last train went a good half hour back. Weather, see? Everything's closing down early."

Eli turned to a chunky guy emerging from a side door, which he locked behind him.

"I need to get to Stockwell."

"Not by tube, you ain't. Other side of London, init? Better get a cab, or start walking, 'cos the buses 'ave stopped too. Happy Christmas."

The transport worker gave him a grin, which looked more like a sneer, as he waddled over to a car that had pulled up and was honking its horn. A moment later the car, and the guy, had gone, leaving Eli alone on the deserted street.

Walk? It'd take him until New Year to get back to Benny's place, and there was no point trying to find a cab because he'd only taken enough money from the change jar to pay for a one way tube ticket. He pressed his head against the cold, hard railing, bracing himself to face the long, freezing walk because he had no other choice.

But you do have another choice... The little voice in his head tumbled down his backbone, making him shiver.

No, he didn't. He couldn't go back to Grey's. He had pride, shredded and tattered though it felt.

Eli's grip on the railings tightened. He should go, make a move, but his legs, like his heart, were as heavy as lead.

How could he have been so foolish as to believe Grey felt anything more than pity and ill-founded responsibility for him? Eli didn't need anybody claiming responsibility for him, he didn't need anybody to hold him up or to take some of the weight that seemed so often to drag him down. He'd be his own strength and support and stand on his own two feet the way he'd always done. He didn't need anybody — he didn't need *Grey* — to keep him upright when sometimes all he wanted was to sink to his knees.

Eli squeezed his eyes tight to stem the threat of hot, salty tears. He shook his head hard, to dislodge the nagging little voice calling him out for the liar that, in his heart, he knew himself to be.

Eli looked up, and snowflakes hit him in the face.

"Oh, fucking hell."

Could the universe get any more shitty? The dark sky had been clear when he'd left, and there hadn't been a breath of wind, but now the clouds had gathered and were dumping all over him, as a brisk and biting wind buffeted him from all sides. Shivering, Eli turned away from the empty, locked-up station, head bowed to make his long, slow way across the city.

Eli trudged along the street, deserted save for the occasional hardy soul, their head down against the rising wind, clutching shopping bags with last minute purchases, and taking no notice of him.

The street was filled with shops and cafés, but most were closed, or getting ready to close, with signs in the windows wishing their customers a Merry Christmas. All around him, the city was literally shutting up shop, getting ready for festivities he'd have no part in, as he made his slow, freezing way towards an empty, cold house on the other side of London.

The snow tumbled down, thicker and heavier; the wind picked up, fierce and blustery, encasing Eli in a blizzard. The snow battered against the bare skin of his face, hundreds of tiny, icy pinpricks. He tugged at the scarf, the soft emerald green scarf Grey had bought as a gift—

"It's just a bloody scarf," Eli muttered, his voice catching, as he wound it around the lower half of his face, but it was soon soaked with the wet snow and he pulled it off and bundled it into the too big coat that still held a trace of Grey's spicy orange cologne.

Eli's vision misted and he dragged the back of one hand across his eyes. It was the snow, that was all it was; his eyes were just watering, he wasn't crying, it had nothing to do with Grey and what Eli had stupidly, ridiculously, pathetically thought might have been happening between them. Because nothing had been happening. Because Grey was still in love with Peter. Because all *he* had been was a diversion, somebody to keep Grey company over Christmas when the only company Grey really wanted was the man he'd spent fifteen fucking years of his life with.

What chance did nothing more than a few days have against that?

I should have left a note... A spasm of guilt shivered through Eli. Whatever delusions Eli had fed himself, Grey had been good to him. Shelter, food, the clothes, but he'd been good to Eli in other ways. Grey had reached inside of him, shining a light on what Eli needed and craved, needs and cravings he'd always kept locked away deep inside, barely acknowledged or understood. The tears began to flow once more, but this time Eli didn't wipe them away as he stumbled along, head down, fighting his way through a world that was growing darker and colder by the second.

"What the...?"

Eli jumped as a spray of wet snow hit him on one side of his face, as a large van on the otherwise empty road drove past. He stopped walking and wiped away the slushy mess.

Looking around him, Eli's stared in dismay. He'd gone the wrong way, the wrong bloody way. His stumbling walk had taken him further, not nearer to his destination, as in front of him, cloaked in beautiful, snowy desolation and stretching for miles, lay Hampstead Heath. The Heath, where he and Grey had hunted down greenery for the living room, where they'd had a snowball fight — and where Grey had saved him from falling, scooping him up in his arms and holding him tight.

Eli covered his face with his hands. He'd never get home, because he had no home to get back to, so what was the point of even trying? As the snow beat down on him from a cold, unfeeling sky, as the wind whipped and grabbed at the coat that still held a taunting trace of Grey, Eli's legs buckled beneath him and he sank to the ground.

Eli didn't know how long he sat there, whether it was one minute, or ten, or an hour. He didn't know anything until he was lifted up by arms which wrapped themselves around him and hugged him tight to a strong chest, where a heart beat its hard, steady rhythm. Shouldn't he struggle, shouldn't he try and get away, and make his cold and lonely journey across a deserted, dark city...? But the words he should say were as frozen as the world around them as he looked up into Grey's serious face.

"It's no use running away, because I'll always find you. I'm taking you back to where you belong. I'm taking you home, little elf."

CHAPTER TWENTY-SIX

"Hot chocolate with marshmallows."

Grey placed the huge mug on the coffee table, and sat down next to Eli, who was curled up in the corner of the sofa, thanking every god he could think of that Eli was home and safe.

He'd driven around in mounting panic, searching the empty streets when he'd found the tube station dark and locked up. Grey had been sick with worry, his heart almost bursting through his rib cage when he'd spotted Eli, collapsed on the frozen ground. Now, all he wanted to do was to hold Eli tight in his arms and never let him go, but first he needed to put right what had gone wrong, and make Eli believe in every word he had to say to him.

"Thank you," Eli said, his voice small and shaky.

"You're lucky I found you, because the weather's lethal." Grey looked over at the window, and the snow hammering against the pane. However long it had taken, Grey would never have stopped searching for him. "Christ, Eli. Why did you run away?" The words exploded from

Grey, all his self restraint collapsing. *Why didn't you give me a chance to tell you what I needed to?*

Eli, head bowed forward, didn't answer, as he sat with his legs pulled up tight against his body, his arms wrapped around his knees.

He looks so young and vulnerable…

"I won't — can't — be a substitute. For Peter."

Eli's quiet words smashed into Grey.

"What? No, of course you're not that. You have to believe me. Me and Peter, we're finished, over. We're divorced. He's met—"

"Somebody else. I know. I know all the facts, but it doesn't stop you from… from loving him still, does it? In here." Without looking up, Eli pressed a hand against his heart. Grey had never seen anything as sad and desolate and every part of him cried out in pain for how wrong Eli had got it.

Grey leaned into Eli and with one finger tilted his chin up, forcing Eli to meet his gaze. Grey's heart stuttered as he stared into those incredible eyes, eyes he'd seen sparkle with life, or widen to dark fathomless pools as their bodies had flowed and melted into each other's. Eyes that had looked into Grey's with a wonder as all those needs and wants Eli was only beginning to comprehend began to unfold in the shadowy places within him.

"You need to listen to me, Eli. You need to listen and understand."

"What's there to under—"

Grey pressed his forefinger to Eli's lips, halting his words. Eli fell silent, and Grey let his hand drop away.

"Just listen to me, okay?"

Eli hesitated, before he nodded.

Silently, Grey counted to three before he spoke.

"Peter turning up today, it was a shock. Other than the phone call, I haven't seen or heard from him in months. He's moved on with his life, and I'm pleased for him. A week or so ago I wouldn't have said that, but I'm saying it now because it's true. I'll always be fond of him, I can't deny that. But love him? Want him by my side? Want him to be the last man I see before I fall asleep, and the first when I wake up? Want him to be the man who completes me, and the man *I* complete? Once, yes. But now? No. No way."

Grey shook his head, the idea that Peter could fill that place, could be the man Grey enfolded in his arms to keep safe, it was wrong, so, so wrong.

"He's not who I want in my life, Eli."

"Isn't he?" Eli whispered. "But I saw you. How you looked at each other. The way the two of you smiled, you —you seemed so happy. And fifteen years together. All that history. How could I ever compete with that?"

"Oh, Eli." Grey cupped his palm over Eli's cheek, a smile ghosting his lips when Eli pushed into the touch without thought or hesitation. His little elf, who needed all the care he could give. "It was my fault. I should have talked to you properly, instead of chewing over Peter's visit and leaving you to put two and two together and come up with five."

Eli ceased nuzzling into Grey's palm, and frowned.

"You were quiet and distant afterwards. You were thinking about what you and he were together. I know you were. There was no place for me. I can't and won't be a second best."

"Second best? No, never. But you're right about one

thing. I was thinking. Not about Peter but about what he said to me. I had to think it through and admit it first to myself before I could admit it to you. The problem was, I took too long over it and before I could say everything I needed to I—I fell asleep. When I woke up, you were gone."

"What do you mean?" Eli's voice was the barest of whispers as he gazed up at Grey.

"Can't you guess?" Grey leaned down, his lips no more than a breath away from Eli's. "Can't you guess, my little elf?"

Lips melted against lips, as soft and sweet as marshmallow laced chocolate. In the grate, the replenished logs glowed a deep, rich red and gold, and the soft lamplight cast its honey glow over them. Grey pulled back from the kiss he wanted to last forever, but there were more words to be said, words which burned deep in Grey's heart. Leaning his forehead against Eli's, Grey said the words that would change his and Eli's life forever.

"I love you, Eli. I think I did from the moment I saw you staring up at me as you hid in the car. My head told me to leave you at your front door and go, and never look back. But my heart whispered no. I couldn't do it. I couldn't leave you out in the cold then, and I can't do it now. I want and need to keep you warm, safe and protected, but I can only do that if it's what you want, too. Is it, Eli? Is it what you want?"

Grey's heart thundered in his chest, as out of control as Eli himself had been as he'd hurtled down the snow-covered Heath. If Eli said no, if he couldn't bring himself to believe, if he shook his head and pulled away…

"You know it's what I want. I... I think you know it more than I do."

Grey eased back and gazed at Eli, at the faint blush colouring Eli's cheeks. Eli dipped his head for a second before he looked up, his gaze sure and steady.

"It is what I want. With you. Only you. For always." Eli smiled and his eyes, his incredible, stunning eyes sparkled with life, and Grey's heart danced.

Only you... For always...

Grey stood and gathered Eli up into his arms, his heart thrilling to Eli's deep, contented sigh as he melted into Grey's strong, sure hold.

"Love you, too."

Grey smiled and his heart sang at the muffled words, whispered against his chest. Holding Eli tight, and never wanting to let him go, Grey carried his best Christmas gift, past, present and future, his very own little elf, upstairs to bed.

EPILOGUE
SIX MONTHS LATER

"Oh, god."

Eli just managed to stop himself from gagging. Turning aside, and as discreetly as he could, he slipped the canapé from his mouth to the napkin and glanced around the crowded terrace, relieved not to encounter outraged glares from his fellow wedding guests. He took a swig from his flute of chilled champagne to wash away the taste of vinegary mustard, chorizo and — peanut? Young waiters and waitresses buzzed around, holding aloft dainty morsels for which, Eli noticed, there were few takers.

"Should have offered pizza bites, or mini jacket potatoes," he muttered to himself.

"I saw that."

A pair of strong arms wound their way around Eli's waist and pulled him in tight against a firm and muscular body, a body Eli had had a lot of fun getting reacquainted with earlier that morning. He had, after all, been away overnight, which had felt like a lifetime supporting, as a favour to his mum and dad, a vegan food festival run by one of their friends. It was the longest time he'd spent away from Grey, and there was no way he was going to be repeating it any time soon.

"Canapé, gentlemen?" A smiley young waiter, gliding up to them, asked.

"No, thank you," Eli and Grey said in unison, looking at each other and laughing. The waiter's curious glance shifted from one to the other before he went on his way.

Eli stepped out of Grey's embrace and looked up at his man.

His man... It was exactly who Grey was, and always would be.

Two little words, they had the power to make his heart beat faster and his mouth water. His man, in his dark blue suit, an exact match to his eyes, was stunning, gorgeous, breathtaking — and all his.

Eli shuffled closer and linking his hands around Grey's neck pulled him in for a long, languorous kiss, his heart skipping and his stomach fluttering as Grey sighed and tightened his hold; Eli's breath hitched as Grey's arousal pressed against him.

"Do you think anybody will miss us if we just slip away?" Eli murmured against Grey's lips.

"Don't tempt me." Grey's voice was rough and raspy, and Eli shivered. "But I suspect David would and—"

A loud, exaggerated cough was a reminder they were not alone.

"David would what?" The chunky guy with bright red hair and a close cropped beard gave them both a big, beaming smile. "Send out a search party? Cut your balls off for abandoning your oldest and best friend on the day of his nuptials? Make you talk to his new father-in-law about mortgages, insurance, and home improvement loans?"

"Lead me to him, if he can get me a better deal on business insurance for Super Spud," Eli said with a grin.

"I'm sure that can be arranged." David gave a serious nod before his face broke out into another wide smile.

Eli listened as David and Grey chatted, interspersed with lots of laughter. The affection between the two friends was as clear as the summer sky above. Eli's attention began to drift, and with a quick kiss to Grey's cheek and a squeeze of his hand, he left them to catch up.

Eli snagged another flute of champagne, and took a chance on another canapé which, this time, didn't need to be deposited into a paper napkin. Winding his way through the assembled guests, he found a space against the far end of the balustrade, partially hidden by a large potted ornamental shrub, and gazed out over the golf course.

The day was growing warmer, and Eli loosened his tie a little. The silk was smooth against his fingers, just as his pale duck egg blue silk shirt was, and so too the soft, fine wool of his dark grey suit, handmade for him just as the shirt was. He leaned forward, clutching the stem of the glass and stared out, unseeing, over the landscaped course.

Sometimes, Eli felt he had to pinch himself, to remind him the life he now lived was truly real. His ambition to start his own business had been achieved. Eli smiled as he recalled Grey's frustration when he'd refused outright to let Grey buy him his mobile catering wagon, or a new van to transport it. This was his venture, he'd told Grey, and he needed to make it happen himself.

Searching the internet, Eli had found somebody who had both a wagon and a small van to sell, both perfect for him. They'd been a good price, but he'd got a much better one for letting Grey do the negotiation. Business was good, with more fairs and festivals in and around London than he could handle. The one small cloud on the clear blue sky of his life was his friendship with Benny, which hadn't survived.

Benny hadn't been able to hide his glee when, on the day he and Lenny had returned to the little house in south London, Eli had told him he was moving out there and then. Benny and a grinning Lenny had made themselves scarce as he and Grey had bundled all his possessions into Grey's car, but before leaving the house that had been his home for a couple of years, Eli had 'relocated' Benny's stash of artisan vodka to the boot of the big Range Rover. Eli's lips quirked with the memory; as far as he was concerned, he was owed.

Eli tipped his face to the warm sun, so different to the bitter winter weather of Christmas Eve, when Grey swept him up in his arms and brought him home, a home Eli had never left and that was now his as much as it was Grey's.

"Hello, Eli."

Eli jumped, sloshing some of his Champagne; he'd been so caught up in his thoughts he hadn't noticed Peter come up beside beside him.

"It's good to see you. I was hoping to be able to have a chat, but best man duties have kept me busy."

How can he be David's brother?

The two men were so different in appearance it was almost laughable. Breathtaking. It really was the only word to describe Peter, but the stomach plummeting inferiority Eli had felt when he'd opened the door to the former model and very much former Mr. Gillespie was as far away as that freezing winter's day.

"Hi, Peter. You're looking well."

Eli didn't know which was the more dazzling, Peter's big, sunshine filled smile or his perfect teeth, glowing white against his golden tanned skin. Peter swept his fingers through his lustrous dark hair. In his suit that fitted like a second skin, the man looked every inch the fashion model he'd once been. It didn't bother Eli one bit because whatever advantages Peter had in this world, he'd lost the one that really and truly mattered.

"I am. Life is good. For all of us, I think."

They fell into silence, both of them looking out over the golf course. Eli sipped his drink, casting furtive glances at Peter. The man hadn't stumbled upon him by accident and, as Peter shifted from foot to foot and scratched the back of his neck, Eli waited for him to say whatever it was he'd sought him out for.

"I was talking to Grey earlier, just for a few minutes, but it was all I needed. I wanted to say thank you."

"What?" Eli's whole body jerked, Peter's words taking him aback. He hadn't known what to expect Peter to say, but it hadn't been this. "Sorry, I don't understand."

"Don't you?" Peter's eyes locked on Eli's. "I've never seen him so content." He paused, as though taking a moment to work out what he was going to say next.

"He's so happy, it just shines from him. It's as though he's found the missing piece of himself — a piece ultimately I couldn't give him. You're that piece, Eli, and I'm glad of that. So, so glad. Grey will always have a special place in my heart, and to see him so complete and content..." A flush washed over Peter's face. "That's all I wanted to say, really." His lips twisted in an awkward smile before he regained his composure. "You've got a very special man in Grey, very special, but I think you already know that."

Peter cocked his head to the side before looking over his shoulder.

"Ah, I can hear my name being called. Best man duties are set to resume." With a quick smile, Peter was gone.

Eli leaned against the balustrade, letting the old, sun warmed stone take his weight. Peter's words, although unexpected, weren't news to him. Eli knew, in his blood, bones, in every part of him, he completed Grey as much as Grey completed him. They were two sides of the same coin, the last two pieces of a jigsaw puzzle that slotted into place, making it whole. Each were night to the other's day, winter to summer, spring to autumn.

You've got a very special man in Grey...

Eli finished up his champagne and pushed away from the balustrade. Special didn't even begin to describe what and who Grey was to him, and would always be.

Making his way back across the terrace, Eli was determined to find his very special man.

"Please don't make me dance," Grey whined when Eli grabbed his hand and tried to pull him to his feet.

"But it's the last dance and our chance to get all romantic. Come on. I promise to let you squeeze my arse — how's that for an inducement? If you don't have this dance with me, I'll let Samantha's cousin Barry have it."

"Like fuck you will." Grey jumped up, his voice a low growl.

He peered across the shadowy dance floor, frowning hard when his eyes found Barry.

The guy had been friendly, *over* friendly, holding onto Eli's hand for too long when they'd been introduced, standing way too close, finding excuses to seek Eli out... It had taken all of Grey's will power not to shove the guy away, that along with Eli's whispered *'easy tiger'*.

On the dance floor, Grey wrapped his arms around Eli, his frown replaced by a smile as Eli leaned into him and sighed.

Slowly, they swayed to the music, a sultry bluesy number. Dipping his head, Grey nuzzled at Eli's soft, silky hair before placing a light kiss on the top of his head.

In the six months they'd been together, they'd slowly met each other's friends, and had even made the long journey to meet Eli's parents on their island home; they'd been wonderful, welcoming and loving and as dippy hippy as Eli had said they were. But, the wedding was the first time they'd been at a large event as a couple. Eli, ever bright and breezy, had denied he was nervous, but Grey had seen through him and had done everything in his power to allay those nerves and put a big, and sated, smile on his face.

"Happy, little elf?" Grey murmured into Eli's hair.

His little elf... A pair of incredible, stunning, beautiful eyes had stared up at him from the foot well of a car, and Grey's life had been changed forever. Thank god Colin had left the door unlocked; maybe the guy deserved a bonus.

"More than you could ever know. I had no idea what happiness was, not until I met you."

Snuggled against Grey's chest, Eli's voice was muffled, but they were clear enough to pierce Grey's heart. What was true for Eli was true for him, too, and he closed his eyes against the sudden sting of tears.

Happy. It was what he was, for the first time in his life. Bone deep, soul drenching happiness, without the vaguest, faintest whisper that something hadn't, quite, clicked or slotted into place. Together he and Eli, his little elf, were a seamless whole; it was hard to know where one of them ended and the other began.

The music faded, then stopped. The last dance was over.

"Ready to go home, little elf?"

Eli gazed up, a soft smile lifting his lips, and Grey's heart soared.

"Home. Yes, I like the sound of that. Always, and forever."

Linking hands, they made their way into the warm summer night and climbed into the back of the car, ready and waiting to take them home.

Home, where it was him and Eli.

Always, and forever.

Thank you for reading Daddy's Christmas Elf — it was a pleasure to share Eli and Grey's story with you.

If you enjoyed Daddy's Christmas Elf, please take a moment to write a review on Amazon, Goodreads, and BookBub.

Why not subscribe to my newsletter? It's chatty, irreverent and contains lots of work in progress updates, plus news of promotions and sales — there's also a juicy sweet with heat free story waiting for you! You can subscribe at me website, where you will also find a full list of all my books:

www.ryecart.com

A FEW WORDS FROM ALI

If you like UK-set contemporary MM romance, I've got you covered.

If you enjoy heartfelt Christmas stories with all the feels and fuzzies, you might want to check out His Perfect Christmas Gift, Christmas Spirit, The Boss of Christmas Present, and Company for Christmas.

If small town romance is your thing, my Love's Harbour series (more books coming!) is for you.

Do you like angsty, gritty stories about love affairs which aren't always pretty? Then take a look at my Rent Boys and Urban Love series.

What about found family stories featuring strong, got-your-back friendships? My Barista Boys series will quench your thirst.

Or maybe a series which follows one adorable couple all the way to their happy ever after? You need to read my Rory & Jack series.

Do you enjoy the thrill of romantic suspense? Something to send a chill down your spine? Look no further than my Deviant Hearts series.

If you'd like find out more about me and my books, visit my website at www.ryecart.com.

I also have a readers group on Facebook, which is mainly where I hang out on social media. Come and join me!

Ryecart's Rebel Readers

Printed in Great Britain
by Amazon

13492244R00122